FALCON'S EGG

FALCON'S EGG ～

by Luli Gray

HOUGHTON MIFFLIN COMPANY

Boston

I have taken some liberties with the architecture of the
American Museum of Natural History. There is no roof
garden in the southeast tower, and nobody lives there.
None of the characters in this book is real, except of
course, Henry and Egg.

Manufactured in the United States of America
Book design by David Saylor
The text of this book is set in 13-point Weiss.
BP 10 9 8 7 6 5 4 3

Library of Congress Cataloging-in-Publication Data
Gray, Luli.
Falcon's egg / by Luli Gray.   p.   cm.
Summary: Taking care of her younger brother and a loving
but flighty mother has made Falcon very responsible for
an eleven-year-old, but she needs the help of her great-great aunt,
a friendly neighbor, and an ornithologist when she finds
an unusual egg in Central Park.
ISBN 0-395-71128-2
[1. Dragons—Fiction. 2. Mothers and daughters—Fiction.
3. New York (N.Y.)—Fiction.]   I. Title.
PZ7.G7794Fal   1995
[Fic]—dc20   94-16731   CIP   AC

For Elizabeth McCulloch,
who led the way

FALCON'S EGG

PROLOGUE

*Y*ou could say it began when Great-Aunt Emily was born into a world without airplanes or astronauts, VCRs, or votes for women.

Or you could say it began on the day Falcon was born, red-faced and hitting out with both fists. "Emily Falcon Davies," said Great-Aunt Emily, peering down. "We can't have two Emilies in this family. Why don't you call her Falcon?"

Or maybe it began with once-upon-a-time, before there was a New York City, or an Emily of any kind at all, when the earth was new and there was no word for magic.

But I'm telling this story, and I say it began on a chilly April day, when Falcon was eleven years old, at the western edge of the Great Lawn in Central Park.

CHAPTER ONE

$\mathcal{T}$he scarlet Egg lay half hidden in the long grass, and though the day was misty and full of rain, the air around it shimmered with heat. Falcon crouched before the Egg, wondering, and reached out to touch it, then jerked back. It was almost too hot to hold. She looked around the park to see if anyone was watching, but there weren't many people around, just a few couples walking under umbrellas on the distant path. She took off her shoes and socks, put one sock into the other, and slipped the Egg quickly inside. She knew that you must never take an egg from a nest, but she wasn't sure about eggs without nests; grownups had so many rules that you didn't know about until you broke them. No one saw her put the sock into her red plastic rain hat. She began to walk toward the path, then stopped. She was supposed to meet her mother at Belvedere Castle at two, and it was nearly that now by her birthday watch. The second hand on the watch face moved around as she stared at it, and the heat from the Egg warmed her hand through the hat. Missy had made her put back the beautiful blue robin's egg she had found two years before. What would she say about a big red Egg almost too hot to touch?

Falcon chewed thoughtfully on a fingernail. Then she pulled $3.17 in quarters, dimes, and pennies from her jeans pocket, and walked quickly toward the castle praying that Missy would be late, as usual.

In the castle gift shop, Falcon went to the counter and bought two postcards of a cardinal and a wood-chuck ("Our Park Friends"), an envelope of "Cobra Eggs," and a blue rubber alligator.

"Two seventy-five, please," said the lady behind the counter. Falcon counted out nine quarters and five dimes.

"May I have a shopping bag, please?" she said.

"Oh sure," said the lady, and put everything into the bottom of a big bag that had the Central Park logo and "Made from Recycled Materials" printed on its side.

Falcon thanked the lady and climbed the stairs to the top of the tower.

At the top she had a clear view of anyone approaching the castle. She took everything out of the bag, put the sock in the bottom, and spread the things she had bought over it. Then she put the rain hat over her wet hair, and rolled her jeans down all the way, so the cuffs covered her sockless ankles. Her mother's face, pink with the climb and the rain, appeared at the entrance to the tower.

"Hallo, baby. Sorry I'm late," she said, emerging onto the roof. She gave Falcon a hug scented with breath mints and what Falcon thought of as "the smell of the week." Missy liked to blend her own perfumes from essences she bought at Caswell-Massey, and sometimes the combinations were very strange. This week, though, it was mostly orange and vanilla.

"You smell like a Creamsicle," said Falcon.

Her mother grinned. "Let's go to Rumpelmayer's and eat banana splits till we explode," she said.

"Can't," said Falcon, pulling away. "It's my day for tea with Ardene."

"Oh," said Missy. "I forgot. Well, can't you do that tomorrow?"

"No, we always have tea on Saturday. She's making

Jelly Tots and I bought her cobra eggs and a blue gator."

Missy's mouth went a bit crooked, and then, without looking at Falcon, she said, "We'd better hurry then. God forbid you should miss out on Jelly Tots." She turned and started down the castle steps. Falcon followed, carrying the shopping bag, and knowing she had said the wrong thing.

CHAPTER TWO

*M*issy always walked fast when she was mad, so Falcon had to hurry to keep up. She was out of breath by the time they got to 16 West 77th Street. She and Missy were the only people on the elevator.

"You going to stop off at home or go straight up to Ardene's?" asked Missy.

"Straight up," said Falcon. Missy pushed the buttons for the fourth and fifth floors. They stood staring straight ahead, in an uncomfortable silence, waiting for the doors to close.

Just as Falcon thought they would stand there forever, the doors closed and Missy poked her in the ribs. She turned and saw that her mother's eyes were crossed and her tongue was stuck out so far it touched her nose. Falcon giggled, and crossed her eyes as the elevator stopped at the fourth floor.

Missy stepped out, speaking in a high, silly voice, "*Do* please bring me back a Jelly Flop, dahling."

"Tot," said Falcon. "Tot, tot, tot."

"Oh, tot tot to you too, old thing." Missy walked toward 4B with one hand on her hip, waggling her behind. She never stayed mad for long.

Ardene Taylor opened the door of 5A with a big smile. "Well, look what the rain blew in! Where have you been?"

"In the park. I brought you a present and can I ask you something, a favor, a big favor, a secret?" Falcon set the bag down in the foyer and struggled out of her damp windbreaker.

"A present, a favor, a secret," said Ardene. "That's some tea! Let's get your hair dried off first." She handed Falcon a big towel. "We'll eat, and then have secrets, hmm?"

Ardene's kitchen was big and airy with black-and-white tiles on the floor. Herbs grew on the windowsill, and there was a clean spicy smell from all the good things Ardene cooked. Falcon's nose twitched like a rabbit's and her mouth began to water.

"Let's see," said Ardene. "Jelly Tots, empanaditas, and Darjeeling with milk, two sugars, right?"

"Right," said Falcon, putting the bag on the counter where she could keep an eye on it while they had tea. She helped Ardene set homemade jam cookies on one plate, tiny meat turnovers on another, and milk and sugar onto a big silver tray. The empanaditas, smelling savory, were out of the microwave in a minute, and tea stood ready in the fat blue pot. The two friends settled on the sofa in the living room, whose windows looked out on the red towers of the Museum of Natural History.

Falcon was hungry. She ate in silence, enjoying the taste of the food. The hot sweet tea warmed her from the inside out. Ardene was the best cook she knew. She had over 400 cookbooks, and she had even written one called *Beside a Namibian Hearth*. Namibia was in West Africa, where Ardene's ancestors had come from more than 300 years ago.

"I do love to see you eat," she said, passing Falcon the empanaditas. Falcon held her mug in both hands to warm them, and smiled up at Ardene's smooth brown face.

"I'll bet your feet are wet," said Ardene. She left the room and came back with a pair of socks. "Take off your shoes, baby, and put these on."

The woolly socks were miles too big. Falcon flexed her toes to make them flop, and felt the warmth creep back into her feet. Ardene poured herself another cup of tea and sat back, curling one leg under the skirt of her green silk dress.

"I brought you some things from the park," said Falcon, and took the cobra eggs and the blue alligator out of the shopping bag.

"Now isn't he cute!" said Ardene, setting the gator on the coffee table. "Uh-oh. What's this? Cobra eggs! I'd better be careful!" She opened the envelope, and dropped it with a shriek as it buzzed and jumped in her hand.

"Got me again!" she said, fanning herself with a napkin. "Scared me half to death." Falcon giggled happily.

"Well now, I've had cobras and alligators, what's the rest?"

Falcon poked at the last cookie on the plate and licked the jam off her finger. Then she lifted the bulging sock from the bag, and set it on the table. Feeling the heat on her hands, she slipped the Egg gently out of the sock onto a crumpled linen napkin. It sat there in the linen nest, twice the size of any hen's egg, glowing like the heart of a burning log.

"Well I'll be," breathed Ardene, and reached out to touch it.

"Wait! It's hot!" said Falcon.

"It is hot!" said Ardene. "What on earth is it? Where did you get it?"

"I found it in the park. It was on the grass. I was afraid it would get broken. Please don't tell." Falcon knelt on the rug with her hands wrapped around the egg.

"Calm down, sweetheart, it's all right. Don't burn yourself, now," said Ardene. She pulled Falcon gently back onto the sofa, cupping her face in one hand. "I guess this is the secret, hmm? And I bet the favor is that I don't tell."

"Well, yes, well sort of but really the favor is, will you keep it here for me so Missy . . . so nobody finds it, keep it safe? Please?"

"Look, sweetheart, as far as I'm concerned this is your egg. If that's what this is. I'm not telling anyone, and I'll keep it here for you if you want, but don't you think we ought to look in the encyclopedia and find out what it is?"

They looked under "eggs," and under "birds" and "reptiles" too, and skimmed through the big illustrated *Birds of the World* for half an hour without success. Falcon sat cross-legged on the rug with *Birds of the World* open to a picture of a wild pheasant. It reminded her of the magical bird in *The Phoenix and the Carpet.* "Maybe this is a phoenix's egg, Ardene!"

"Falcon honey, that's just a story. This thing is real, and it's here now, today." She went to the window and stared out, leaning on the wide sill. Falcon watched her and thought she could almost hear her brain working. She knew that when Ardene Taylor got to thinking hard, something was bound to happen. Suddenly she shouted, "HA!"

Falcon jumped. "What?" she asked.

"The Museum of Natural History, of course, right there across the street. We'll ask them. Who would know better about peculiar eggs?"

Falcon stared out at the huge stone building across 77th Street. Her great-great-aunt Emily always said you could learn about almost anything at the museum. Aunt Emily was friends with several of the people who worked there. "Ardene," Falcon said, "my aunt Emily, she knows someone there, a man who writes about birds, a . . . an . . . orthenologist, I think it is."

"Ornithologist," said Ardene. "What's his name?"

"Freddy," said Falcon. "That's all I know, she calls him Freddy. We'll have to ask her."

"That means telling her about the Egg," said Ardene.

Falcon thought about Aunt Emily's face, how terribly old it looked, the skin so thin you could see blue veins through it, and the eyes pale gray and very clear. She remembered what her aunt had said to her soon after her father had left, when she was six, and her brother, Toody, was about to be born. "Falcon, I am very old and you are very young, but I should like us to be friends." And they were, thought Falcon, even though her great-great-aunt was almost a hundred years old, and Falcon was only eleven. She could say things to Aunt Emily she couldn't say to anyone else: mean, angry things about Toody, or even about Missy. Aunt Emily would sit by the fire that burned even in summer. ("Old bones are full of winter," she said.) And she listened. Somehow, once Falcon said the mean things, they didn't seem so terrible. She could remember the way Missy had special jokes just for her, and the way her mouth looked when she grinned, instead of the shouting before Peter left, and the silence after.

She knew Aunt Emily would keep her secret safe.

"Can you tell her on the phone?" asked Ardene.

Falcon shook her head. "She doesn't hear very well on the phone. You have to shout. She needs to see you to hear." Falcon pressed her chin against her knees to help her think.

They usually visited Aunt Emily on Sundays, all three of them. Missy didn't like going there. She always got fussy before they went. She yanked at their clothes, and brushed Toody's hair so hard that he screamed and got red in the face. By the time they left, Toody was cranky, and Missy was walking with hard, angry strides. Falcon asked her mother once why they had to go, and she seemed surprised by the question.

"Why, baby, I thought you adored Emily. You're always begging to go; I thought you liked her."

"I do," said Falcon, "but you don't." It was a Saturday morning, and she was sitting on her mother's bed beside the tray of black coffee and toast she'd arranged so carefully. The window blinds were drawn so the room was dim and quiet. Falcon's mother had a migraine, and she lay back on the piled-up pillows with a blue plastic headache mask over her eyes. She always kept two in the freezer. The coldness helped, she said, and so did strong coffee, and darkness. Missy took off the mask. Her face looked sad with yesterday's makeup still on it, the mascara smudged and the lipstick worn off.

"I do like her," she said. "We used to be good friends. But lately, I don't know." Missy sighed. "She's the only relative I have, and she was so kind to me when I was married and alone in New York."

Falcon didn't see how you could be alone if you were married, but she knew better than to ask about that, or to remind her mother of her father when she had a headache. So she said, "I'm your relative and so is Toody." Her mother put the mask on, and lay back against the pillows.

"Yes you are, baby. Coffee's lovely. Thanks."

Falcon was almost sure her mother would let her go to Aunt Emily's with Ardene. "Would you go with me tomorrow if Toody and Missy don't come?"

"Sure, honey," said Ardene. "We'd better bring the Egg."

Falcon looked at it, glowing in its linen nest, and shook her head. She knew that she would feel better if the Egg stayed here, at Ardene's. "If you move an egg from its nest, the mother bird won't take care of it," she said.

Ardene looked at the Egg and then at Falcon. "And I suppose you are the mother bird, is that right?"

"Sort of," said Falcon.

"Well, maybe you are at that. I have an idea." Ardene left the room and came back with a huge furry hat lined in quilted brown satin. She said it was from Russia, and had belonged to her late husband, William. He had never worn it because he thought it looked silly. Ardene chuckled. "It did, too, made him look like a hairy mushroom."

Falcon had seen the wedding picture beside Ardene's bed. Ardene wore a white, gauzy dress, and she towered over William, who stood beside her, gazing not at the camera, but at her. He had died the year before Falcon was born, which was hard to imagine. How could the world be without her to know it?

She watched as Ardene took the Egg and carefully placed it inside the fur hat, which almost completely enveloped it.

"There!" she said. "That's safe and private and warm." She smiled at Falcon, who wrapped her arms as far as they would go around Ardene's green silk self, and hugged her hard.

CHAPTER THREE

𝓕alcon's mother was home. She almost never went out on Saturday night. She said there were too many people. So she went to the theater or out to dinner on Tuesdays or Thursdays or Fridays, and then slept late, while Falcon got breakfast for herself and Toody, shushing him so as not to wake Missy.

On Saturday nights she stayed home, and they sent out for Chinese food or pizza, and played Clue. Sometimes they painted pictures with Missy's colored pencils and watercolors, the same ones she used for work. Falcon had every book her mother had illustrated, in the bookcase her father had built. She didn't read them very often because they made her think of Deadlines.

Each time her mother had a book to do, she got

excited. She woke up early and put on clean jeans and a T-shirt to make breakfast. She hugged Toody and Falcon before they got into the van that took them to school, and picked them up where the van stopped in the afternoon, walking fast in her red running shoes, full of beans. Beans were what they usually had for dinner, in those times: beans, brown rice, spaghetti, salad, and fruit from Greenmarket for dessert. Falcon wasn't crazy about all those vegetables, but it was worth eating them for the happy look on her mother's face.

Then, after a month or so, Missy would start to talk about the Deadline. "Deadline" was a scary word that made Falcon think of people standing in line to die, and it made her mother more and more nervous. She went to late movies and took all-night walks, and slept all morning. Falcon and Toody walked back from where the van dropped them after school in the afternoon, and Missy would be in her studio, in a flannel nightie and yesterday's makeup, squinting through her glasses at them as though they were strangers, or even burglars.

"Send out for something, or there's PB and J. Don't stay up late, babes. Now be good and don't fuss. I've got this damn Deadline." She thrust a hand through her hair and turned back to the easel, scowling at the sheet of paper pinned there.

At Deadline time, Falcon and Toody watched TV until late at night. Toody liked cooking shows and *Night Court,* and so did Falcon, but she liked *Masterpiece Theater* most of all, and anything with Bill Moyers. She was sure that if you had Bill Moyers around, nothing very bad could happen. Usually Toody fell asleep on the sofa with Henry Cat wrapped around his head, and Falcon went to bed by herself. She didn't even brush her teeth, until Ardene told her, "Take care of your teeth and your feet, Falcon. As long as you can eat and walk, you'll be fine." So she flossed and brushed and rinsed, every night. She tried to make Toody do it too, but he liked to pull all the floss out of the dispenser and wrap it around his finger to make the tip get fat and red, and he used so much toothpaste he looked like a mad dog in a cartoon.

Sometimes it made her sad going to bed with no one to tuck her in, but she felt better when Henry jumped on the bed, walking all over her to find just the right spot. He purred as he curled up behind her knees, and once he was settled in she fell asleep easily.

This Saturday was at the beginning of a Deadline, so Missy was only a little jumpy. She still made a real dinner, even though there was a cup of coffee beside her plate of whole-wheat pasta instead of juice. Falcon ate all her dinner: gummy spaghetti, sandy salad, and rusty apple slices with yogurt. She said it was delicious, and hoped Toody wouldn't complain, but he was hungry after his play group, and gobbled the whole meal with hardly a word.

"I'll clean up," said Falcon.

"Thanks, babe, you're a peach. I've got a load of work. Don't stay up too late, hmm?" said her mother, heading toward the studio.

"Missy," said Falcon quickly, "could I take Ardene to see Aunt Emily tomorrow, just us, and maybe you could take Toody to the zoo?"

"Oh. Well, I guess so, sure, why not. I had enough of her last weekend." Actually it was two weeks ago, but Falcon wasn't going to argue.

She dialed Ardene's number, and said in a growly voice, "This is Egg Command. All systems go for Sunday." Ardene laughed.

"Well, the child has finally lost her mind," she said. "I'll pick you up at quarter to eleven then, Admiral?"

"Roger. Over and OUT," said Falcon. She hung up and went into the kitchen to clean up. She was in such a good mood that she let Toody put the silver away even though he smeared it with his dirty fingers and made too much noise with the spoons. She even made a bubble bath for him, and let him brush his teeth in the tub. She read to him from *In the Night Kitchen* when he was in bed with his fuzzy duck. "Milk in the batter! milk in the batter! we bake cake and nothing's the matter!" chanted Toody, who knew it by heart.

Just before she fell asleep with Henry under the covers beside her, she thought of the Egg in its fur nest, dark and warm. She hugged Henry, who stretched, and curled into a ball with a paw over his nose. "Just like us, Cat," she whispered. "Nothing's the matter."

CHAPTER FOUR

$\mathcal{F}$alcon was up early next morning, washed and dressed in her navy corduroy jumper, with a clean white blouse and socks with only one hole in the heel. (It didn't show if she didn't pull them all the way up.) She had fed Toody and herself on stale raisin bran, and he was planted in front of the TV. Her mother was still asleep. Falcon sat on the sofa, thinking about the Egg. She could see it in her mind: warm, glowing, perfect. She wondered what her aunt would say, and what an ornithologist would be like.

At 10:40 the doorbell rang, and there stood Ardene in her bright yellow raincoat. Falcon slipped out before Toody saw her; she didn't want him begging to come too. Ardene raised her eyebrows as Falcon closed the door very quietly.

"It's okay. Missy's home and Toody's watching *Face the Nation*." She didn't say Missy was still asleep, and she wasn't sure if that was okay, but she pushed the thought to the back of her mind and got into the cab with Ardene.

It was starting to drizzle as they drove through the park, and raining hard by the time they arrived at Aunt Emily's building on East 66th Street. There was a long wait after Falcon rang the doorbell of number 12, and then her great-great-aunt opened the door, leaning on her silver-topped cane. "Good morning!" she said. "Good morning!" she said again when she saw Ardene. "Ms. Taylor, good morning. How lovely to see you."

"Good morning, Ms. Meade, how are you?" said Ardene. Falcon said good morning too, which was five good mornings, and they weren't even inside yet.

"Quite a surprise, and a fine one too," said Aunt Emily, showing them in. "Falcon, would you like to make us some coffee?"

"Yes please," said Falcon, and went into the kitchen to turn on the coffee machine. She could hear Ardene and Aunt Emily talking in the living room, but she couldn't hear what they were saying.

She put three flowered cups on a tray. They were so thin you could see light through them, and they went "ping" when you flicked them with a fingernail. Or when Aunt Emily did—Falcon's nails were bitten too short to flick. Once, when she was seven, she had broken one of the cups. Her mother had been very angry, and had scolded her as she mopped cocoa off the rug and picked up the pieces of porcelain.

Aunt Emily had said, "Don't carry on so, Margaret. Porcelain is nothing but baked mud, and everything breaks sooner or later. Falcon, get another cup, and have some cocoa. It's perfectly all right." Missy's face had gone very red but she had gotten Falcon a fresh cup of cocoa herself, and went to sit by the window with Toody in her lap, while Falcon and Aunt Emily talked about the dinosaurs at the Museum of Natural History.

Falcon carried the tray of coffee into the living room very carefully and set it down on the table beside Aunt Emily's chair. She was proud of herself. The coffee was just right, with hot foamy milk on top, no scum, and not a drop in the saucers. "Delicious!" said Aunt Emily.

"Yes indeed!" said Ardene. "Well."

"Well," said Aunt Emily. There was a long silence. Falcon's father, Peter, said there was a silence every twenty minutes in any conversation. It was a theory that Falcon kept meaning to test, but she always forgot about it until the conversation was over.

At last Falcon began. "Aunt Emily, yesterday I was in the park, and I found—"

"The park!" interrupted Aunt Emily. "By yourself, I suppose?"

"Well, yes," said Falcon, "on my way to meet Missy, and I found—"

"I've told Margaret a thousand times, it simply is not right, so dangerous nowadays, and you only ten years old, I don't know what she can be thinking."

"Eleven," said Falcon. "I'm eleven, and anyhow I was on the Great Lawn, and I found—"

"Ten, eleven, it makes no difference, it's irresponsible, don't you think, Ms. Taylor?"

"I think," said Ardene, "you might want to hear what Falcon has to say."

"Oh. Well, what is it, Falcon? I'm sorry, I didn't mean to interrupt, it's just that . . . What did you find?"

Falcon gave Ardene a grateful look, and began telling Aunt Emily about the mysterious Egg. Her aunt did listen this time, and when Falcon said the Egg was hot, Aunt Emily started in her chair, and her cheeks grew pink.

"So we thought your friend Freddy might know," said Falcon, finishing her story. "The or-ni-thol-o-gist," she added, saying the word carefully to be sure she got it right.

"Well!" said Aunt Emily. "That's quite a story. Have you got it with you?"

"No," said Ardene. "Falcon thought it needed to be quiet. Private."

"Ah yes. Quite right." Aunt Emily picked up the black leather address book from the table beside her, and slid her finger down the M's. "Here it is," she said. "Fernando Maldonado, home number. Bring me the telephone, would you, child?" Falcon handed her the portable phone, and watched while she pressed the buttons. Aunt Emily's phones had gadgets on them to make them louder, but she still shouted into the mouthpiece as though she would hear better if she made more noise. "Freddy, is that you?" she cried.

A gabbling sound came out of the phone.

"No time for all that," said Aunt Emily. "This is a scientific emergency. Will you come to number sixteen West Seventy-Seventh Street, apartment number . . ." She looked enquiringly at Ardene.

"Number five-A. Taylor," said Ardene.

"Yes, apartment number five-A, Ms. Taylor, in half

an hour?" Falcon heard the word "baseball." "Nonsense!" said Great-Aunt Emily. "This is important. No, I can't. You have to see it. Well, bring an umbrella, it's only just across the street." She hung up. "We're off," she said, looking pleased with herself.

"Maldonado. Doesn't he write for *Natural History* magazine?" said Ardene.

"Yes, he's a clever young man. Very nearly a bird himself . . . if a bird wore unmatched socks and didn't own a comb. Come to think of it, birds don't wear socks. Falcon, don't snort. It's very rude. Let's go."

In no time at all they were bundled into a cab. Falcon was squashed between Great-Aunt Emily in a huge yellow sou'wester, and Ardene in her yellow Burberry. She felt like an egg herself, being sat on by two large yellow hens.

CHAPTER FIVE

$\mathcal{W}$hen they entered the lobby of number 16 with Ardene in the lead, they saw a tall, skinny man struggling to close an umbrella. He had straight, floppy black hair, his pants were too short, and he wore a white sock on one foot and no sock on the other. He looked up from the umbrella, which popped open again. *"Porca Miseria!"* he said. "I'm Fernando Maldonado and this stupid thing won't close."

Ardene took the umbrella, which folded obediently at her touch, and said, "Come on up, Dr. Maldonado. I'm Ardene Taylor. Thank you for coming." Freddy then saw Aunt Emily, and strode toward her, happy to see a familiar face.

"Emily, how are you? Oh, you're Falcon, aren't

you?" He squinted down at her as though she were a new species of bird.

"Emily Falcon Davies," she said, in her most grown-up manner.

In Ardene's living room, they sat around the coffee table with the fur hat in the middle. "We have brought you here," said Aunt Emily, "in your ornithological capacity, to investigate a singular phenomenon which . . ." Here she stopped, and laughed. "Oh dear, there I go. I'm sorry, Falcon, this is your discovery. Won't you tell Dr. Maldonado yourself?"

Falcon had been enjoying the sound of the big words Aunt Emily was using, and the way her hands waved around as she spoke, so it took her a moment to realize that her aunt was speaking to her. She turned to Dr. Maldonado and told him about finding the Egg. "It's hot, see?" She reached out and pushed down the edges of the hat. Dr. Maldonado's dark eyes opened very wide. He gave a low whistle, and touched the Egg gingerly with his fingertips.

"Extraordinary," he said, staring. "So remarkably hot. The size. Extraordinary color, not easily camouflaged. Goose mutation perhaps? Heat, though, quite improbable. I wonder . . ."

Aunt Emily leaned toward the egg, feeling its heat

on her face. Her eyes were full of wonder, and for a moment she looked almost young. Then she sat back, and said, "Well, Freddy, this is a remarkable scientific discovery. Hadn't you better ascertain what this is, and whether it is viable? If it is, then we must decide what is to be done with it."

"I found it," said Falcon, in a small voice, but no one heard her.

Dr. Maldonado felt around in his pockets, and said he needed his stethoscope. He looked around the living room as though he thought he might find one there. Ardene went into the kitchen, and came back holding a tiny metal cone with an oddly shaped opening at the small end. She said it was a pastry bag tip, for making roses out of icing, and held it out to the ornithologist. He looked at it doubtfully, but took it, and crouched down before the egg. Leaning over it, he put the narrow end of the cone to his ear and the wide end right against the Egg.

They all held their breaths. Freddy sat back on his heels. "I think so," he said. "It's faint, but steady. I think it's alive."

"Do you mean it's going to hatch?" asked Ardene.

"It might. I think so. Maybe," he said.

"How long?" said Falcon.

"Oh, eleven centimeters, I think, maybe twelve."

"No, I mean how long will it take to hatch?" asked Falcon.

"Oh. Well." He shrugged. "I have no idea, but the heartbeat is . . . maybe a few weeks? I don't really know."

"We'll just have to wait and see then," said Ardene. "Dr. Maldonado, do you think the Egg is safe here, as it is, in the hat? Do you think I should put a heating pad under it, to keep it warm?"

Freddy looked anxious. "Don't think so. Seems to generate its own heat: singular, very. Safe enough, though. Of course, laboratory conditions, facilities, at the museum, you know. X-ray, to see what it might be; perhaps we should . . ."

It seemed to Falcon that none of the grownups knew any more about it than she did herself and, after all, she had found it. "It's my Egg," she said loudly. All three heads turned toward her. "It shouldn't go all over the place, and have people poking at it and asking questions."

Great-Aunt Emily stared at Falcon, who stood with her fists clenched and her face as red as the Egg. "I think the child is right."

Ardene nodded. "I think so too. An egg needs to be kept safe."

Freddy stopped chewing his knuckle and looked

relieved. "Safe. Yes. Precisely. That hat, or . . . nest. Yes."

"It has to be a secret," hissed Falcon, "or people will bother it, hurt it. We have to take care of it. We have to be . . ." She knew what she meant to say, but not how to say it.

"We have to be its friends," said Great-Aunt Emily.

"Yes!" said Falcon. "That's it."

"So," said Ardene, "that's what we'll be then: the Friends of Egg."

They all said the words, turning them over on their tongues: "The Friends of Egg."

"We should swear a Bloody Oath!" said Falcon. "A blood bond never to speak the Great Name of Egg, and . . ."

"Don't be lurid, Falcon," said Great-Aunt Emily. "There's no need for such nonsense."

Falcon kept quiet, but she still thought it was a good idea.

CHAPTER SIX

$\mathcal{E}$arly spring is a time of waiting. In the country, there are eggs ready to hatch, and lambs about to be born. Farmers plant corn and lettuce and beans, and wait for them to poke their pale green shoots up through the damp earth. Children sniff the air, fidget at their desks, and wait for the school day to end. In New York City, the streets are cleared of the last gray slush. People open their coats to the April wind and catch the smell of lilacs from the Conservatory Garden at 105th Street, waiting for picnics, and vacations by the sea. And, at number 16 West 77th Street, the Friends of Egg waited too.

All through the spring, they met in 5A when they could, to sit around the fur hat and watch. Freddy Maldonado brought his stethoscope and reported that the Egg's heartbeat was growing stronger, and that its temperature stayed steady at 127° Fahrenheit. Ardene Taylor made cool, fruity milkshakes. Aunt Emily sat in the big rocker, not saying much. She just rocked, watching the Egg, and thinking of long ago, remembering, and wondering.

In 4B, Missy was hard at work on her new book. She didn't cook, and the refrigerator was full of white cardboard cartons of half-eaten moo shu pork, and slabs of leftover pizza. Toody and Falcon stayed up late, watching television, and Toody had nightmares for a week after he saw *Night of the Living Dead*. He went to his play group after school every day, so Falcon usually had time to slip upstairs for an hour or so to sit with the Egg. Ardene had given her a set of keys. "Call before you come up, honey, and lock up when you go."

Missy said, "As long as Ardene doesn't mind, it's fine with me. Just be sure you're back in time to get Toody, please, baby. I've got this Deadline."

At school Falcon daydreamed more than usual, and the other kids began calling her birdbrain.

It wasn't as bad as some of the other names they had called her since the first grade, so she didn't mind, much. The only kids who were really nice to her were Kevin and Lily Weng, and nobody liked Kevin. He had sticky-out ears, and he always came to school in a long-sleeved white shirt with a clip-on bowtie.

Falcon had met Lily Weng in the third grade. She looked so neat with her glossy black hair in two braids, and a sharp crease down each leg of her new blue jeans. The kids made fun of her clothes, and that afternoon Falcon saw her in the girls' room, rubbing her jeans with water and squeezing them to get the crease out.

"What are you doing?" said Falcon.

"My mother ironed my jeans. I told her not to, they look so DUMB," said Lily Weng furiously. After that she wet and crumpled her jeans, and her other clothes too, as soon as she got to school. The first time Falcon went to Lily's house in her not-very-clean red corduroys with the rip in the knee, and her faded orange T-shirt that had had bleach spilled on it by accident, Mrs. Weng looked at her hard. The next day Lily still looked neat, but her jeans were not ironed, and she wore sneakers instead of Mary Janes. And a big smile too, when she saw Falcon.

"My mother said, 'A compromise is in order,'" Lily said.

"What does that mean?" asked Falcon.

"I guess it means I don't have to be ironed," said Lily.

Falcon was glad when June came and school was out for the summer. The first thought in her head when she woke up with the sun on her face was: "NO SCHOOL!!" She lay back and stretched like Henry, who purred and rubbed his cheek against hers as though he were glad too. After breakfast the two of them went up to Ardene's to sit with the Egg. Henry hissed the first time he saw the fur hat, and Falcon stood ready to snatch him away if he started to pounce. She watched him approach it stiff-legged and sideways till he was near enough to sniff it. Then he gave it two quick pats, turned his back, and had a good wash. After that he ignored it. He spent most of his time on the sill above the window-seat, where Falcon sat curled against the cushions, reading, watching the Egg, or just dreaming.

She was always sure to be at Belvedere Castle at two to pick up Toody from his play group, and take him to junior swim, which was taught by Lily Weng's aunt, Mei Chu.

The other kids all had grownups bringing them.

When Mei Chu asked Falcon about her mother, Falcon said, "My mother is very busy on her new book, so she can't bring us. She trusts me—I am very mature for my age."

Mei got a funny look on her face, and said, "You certainly are! Well, I'd like to meet her. Please ask her to phone when she can, will you, Falcon?"

"Oh yes, I will, I'll tell her," said Falcon. After that Mei didn't ask any more questions.

Falcon was a good swimmer, and she would have liked her mother to see how well she dove and swam. But she was glad Missy didn't come. She was so different from the other mothers. They all wore outfits that matched: fancy running clothes or elegant linen slacks. Missy just put on whatever was on the floor by her bed, smelling it first to be sure it was clean, and her clothes were always wrinkled, with ripped hems and ink stains in embarrassing places. Her hair looked like a bird's nest, and she wore just one earring because after she had the first ear pierced she had changed her mind.

And Falcon didn't want Missy to find out that Toody hated the water and never went into the pool at all. He just sat on the edge of the shallow end and kicked his feet. Mei never yelled at him, or tried to make him get in. She showed him how to do the crawl stroke, the side stroke, and the breast stroke with his arms, and he practiced them, standing by the pool. When they first started going to the class he wouldn't even go near the pool, so putting his feet in the water was progress.

Falcon liked Lily's aunt. Mei talked to her and the other kids as though they were people, not with the stupid voice most grownups use when they talk to children. Sometimes Lily Weng came to class, and afterward Falcon went to Lily's house to play, or Lily came to hers, if Missy didn't have a Deadline.

When she didn't, she made up wonderful games. She had a trunk in her bedroom full of old clothes and funny hats, fur-trimmed capes, fake jewelry, and a baggy black woolen costume that had been Aunt Emily's bathing suit when she was a young girl. "How could anyone swim in that?" wondered Falcon.

"I don't know, but they did. Emily's a fine swimmer, even now," said Missy, struggling into a tight red dress with spangles all over the front. Suddenly, she seemed to turn into someone else. "I am the Enchanted Princess Wandafola," she said in a high, fluty voice, dragging a feather boa behind her across the floor.

Then out of the trunk came an old fur coat, and goggles, a big black hat, and a pair of fuzzy blue slippers. Missy swept them up into a story of mad scientists, monsters, and magic that ended with Missy playing "Hail to the Chief" while the others marched around waving a broom, a mop, and a plastic horn. "The forces of Good have triumphed!" announced Missy. "We will have a celebration feast and tame Dr. Creepo with—"

"PIZZA!" shouted Lily, who was Dr. Creepo. It was, she said, "My most favorite food in the entire universe," and something she never had at home. Her parents were very strict, but nice. They never seemed to have Deadlines or Nerves.

The Wengs never let Lily take a bus or cab by herself, or go to the park alone. It made Lily mad.

"Falcon's mother lets her!" she said angrily to her mother.

"These are our rules, Lily," said Helen Weng, calmly, and that was that. Falcon felt sad that day, she didn't know why. After all, she got to go to the park by herself, and take cabs and buses too, though never after dark, and never the subway.

"Too many rats and crazies," said Missy, when Falcon asked.

During Deadline time Falcon didn't see much of Lily. She had to spend all her time with Toody. If it was nice out, she took him to the playground in the park, or to the zoo. When it rained they colored, or Falcon read to him in the shabby old blue chair. He would tuck himself in under her arm so he could see the book, with Henry draped over the back of the chair, bopping them with his tail. Those were the times she liked her brother best, when they were lost in a story with Mr. Toad, or the Borrowers, or Mrs. Tiggywinkle. It felt good to cuddle him, especially when he was all pink and warm and sweet-smelling after his bath.

Falcon wished Toody were old enough to play Scrabble. They played Parcheesi sometimes, but she usually lost her temper. Toody liked to march the pieces around the board yelling, "Boing! Boing! Boing!"

"It's against the rules!" Falcon shouted, snatching his piece away. He tried to grab it back, and ran roaring into the studio, where Missy was working, with her hair stuck full of pencils.

"Oh babies, please," said Falcon's mother. "You're a big girl, Falcon. Be nice to your brother, and we'll go out to dinner, only don't FUSS!"

None of the other kids at Chapman School had to take care of their baby brothers. They all had nannies or au pairs. The au pairs were teenagers from foreign countries who lived with American families and took care of their children.

Falcon and Lily were best friends, though Lily seemed to like all the kids, even the mean ones who called Falcon names. When Lily was around, they stopped the names, but Falcon knew they didn't like her. She had known it from her first day at Chapman. She had been so excited to be starting school, walking into the classroom with her mother and father holding her hands. She sat down at a desk and picked up the book in front of her. "First Reader" it said on the cover. She grinned up at her parents, who looked a little anxious. "Want to wear my lucky tooth?" asked Peter. He took off the leather thong with the fossil tooth he had found in Arizona, and hung it around her neck. "Good times, little bird," he said.

But it wasn't good times. When the teacher, Mrs. Enderberg, found out that Falcon already knew how to read, she was annoyed, and said that Falcon would have to learn all over again, "the right way." So Falcon had to sit in class while they went through the *First Reader*, oh so slowly. The chair under Falcon's bottom grew harder and harder and her jaw ached from trying not to yawn. When recess came, the other kids called her showoff, and picked her last for softball. She wandered off into the outfield, and when she found herself near the gate, she just walked out and took a cab to Aunt Emily's.

The old lady listened to her, dried her tears, and made her a cup of cocoa. Then they sat on the couch and looked through Aunt Emily's photograph albums. There were several brownish pictures of her as a little girl in long loose dresses with a huge bow in her hair. "You looked like me!" said Falcon.

Aunt Emily turned the pages until she came to a large, faded picture of herself looking grown-up and beautiful with flowers in her hair in a lacy dress. She was holding hands with a man in uniform. "That was Charles," she said. "He was my fiancé. He was killed three months after that was taken, in the Great War, flying over France."

"Oh Aunt Emily!" said Falcon, her eyes brimming.

Aunt Emily smiled at her, and slipped a bony arm around her shoulder. "I thought I would die of sadness. But I didn't. I've had a wonderful life. Just look."

They looked at the album for hours, while Emily told stories about the old photographs. There was one of her, with several other people, all dressed in furs and boots, on the side of a mountain. "Climbing in the Himalayas," she said. She pointed at another picture. "On safari in Kenya. In Madrid on assignment for the *World Tribune* in 1936. In Paris signing copies of my book on the Spanish Civil War. That's Picasso waving a copy over his head and grinning."

Aunt Emily helped, and so did Ardene, but Falcon still hated school. Lily was her only friend, and now, in sixth grade, they weren't as close as they had been. Some of the girls at school had been acting very stupid lately, and when Lily was with them, she acted stupid too. They spent all their time giggling and screaming and talking about boys. When Lily came to Falcon's house, she went on and on about Sean Gallatin, who sat next to her in English.

"He's just so cool!" Lily said. Falcon didn't think Sean was cool at all. He was one of the dumbest kids at Chapman. But she didn't say anything.

"What's the matter, don't you like him?" asked Lily.

"He's okay," mumbled Falcon. "You want to play Scrabble?"

"No, I know! Let's try on your mother's makeup," said Lily, who wasn't allowed to do that at home.

Falcon agreed without enthusiasm, and later, when Lily was washing her face before going home, she said, "Maybe on Friday we could go to the Metropolitan with your mother. It's open late."

Lily shook her head, reaching for a towel. She said she was going out to Long Island with Linny Kressler and spending the night. "We're going to Kenwood Mall on Saturday with a bunch of other kids," she said.

"I didn't know you were friends with Linny!" said Falcon.

"Well, I am. She's way cool."

"I think she's mean!" said Falcon hotly.

"Okay, *fine!*" said Lily, and went home.

It wasn't exactly a fight, but after that Falcon knew she didn't want to tell Lily about the Egg.

CHAPTER SEVEN

$\mathcal{B}$y the end of June, New York was unusually hot. Ardene said it was the greenhouse effect. Falcon thought that sounded nice, as though everything would grow, and be fresh and green, but Ardene said it meant that the shield of air around the earth had grown too thin. That was why the sun's rays made things hotter than they should be. And it certainly was hot, and sticky and dirty too.

When Falcon stepped out of number 16 onto the street, the air felt heavy and thick. She went to the Museum of Natural History often, because it was cool and full of shadows, especially in the sea mammals room. She could stand under the great blue whale and imagine herself on the ice with the walrus. There were cool places in the park too, but the coolest place in the city was the pool at junior swim. The clear blue water slid over her bare skin, and even the noise of the other kids disappeared up into the high ceiling.

Sometimes Falcon thought that Mei Chu was really a dolphin in disguise. She swam with hardly a ripple, just curving through the water as easily as though she'd been born there. Falcon's own swimming was much more splashy, but Mei said she was learning fast. She was proud of being able to swim with the eight-pound weight. That was part of the junior life-saving class she was taking, and she was better than anyone else.

Toody had graduated to standing in the shallow end and waving his arms, or holding on to the side and kicking. Now that he wasn't afraid of the water, he liked to make the loudest possible splashes with his feet. Mei Chu told him to keep his elbows high, and said he was doing fine. And Toody called it swimming, which was ridiculous in Falcon's opinion.

The pool was closed over the Fourth of July weekend. Mei Chu and her two partners, Tom and Frank, went to Montauk to stay with Lily's family in their big house on the beach. Falcon had seen pictures of it. Lily's mother had asked her to come for a weekend, but Falcon didn't like the idea of all those people seeing her raggedy pj's, and maybe hearing her make noises in the bathroom.

That was why Falcon didn't have much to do that weekend. Ardene was away. She said Falcon could come by and sit with the Egg, but she couldn't because she had to watch Toody all the time. Her mother hardly ever came out of the studio except to get more iced tea. Even the worst of her perfume mixtures would have been better than the sour, stale smell that hung around her now. She wore the same old cut-off jeans and faded T-shirt all the time, and kept her hair in a greasy ponytail tied with a shoe-lace. All they ate was take-out from the Korean deli on 77th and Columbus.

Falcon began to think it might be a good idea to let Toody in on the secret of the Egg. If he knew, she could take him to Ardene's with her, instead of to the zoo for the millionth time. But she wasn't sure he could keep a secret, and she knew that if Missy found out, Falcon would have to put the Egg back. When she had taken the robin's egg, Missy had said it was like kidnapping.

Falcon and Toody went to Aunt Emily's on Sunday, and Falcon and Aunt Emily did *The New York Times* crossword puzzle together while Toody played with the geodes Aunt Emily had brought back from all over the world. They were dull and gray on the outside, like stone eggs, but their insides were full of glittery crystals of purple, yellow, and blue. Aunt Emily said that in the old days people believed there was magic in jewels, that they could be used to cure illness and bring good or bad luck, or even death. Falcon asked her if that were true. Aunt Emily said the old legends weren't scientifically true. Then she stared into space for a moment, and touched Falcon's cheek. "But the world is full of mysteries. I've lived a long time and the older I get, the more I know how little I know."

That sounded like a riddle to Falcon, but she liked the sound of her aunt's voice, and the look in her pale eyes.

Falcon didn't think Toody should touch the geodes with his grubby hands, but Aunt Emily said, "When all's said and done, they're just rocks, Falcon, and Tudor is a live boy."

"That's dumb," muttered Falcon.

"What's that?" said Aunt Emily.

"Nothing," said Falcon. "I didn't say anything."

At last, on the Tuesday after the Fourth, the pool reopened. Falcon got there extra-early, practically dragging Toody, who wanted to stay home and watch *The Frugal Gourmet*. Mei Chu and Frank were surprised to see them. Class wouldn't start for forty-five minutes, but Mei said they could sit on the bench outside the pool room, which was still locked. She and Frank were in the office doing paperwork.

Falcon went over to look at the swimming team records that hung on the wall by the bench. There were pictures of big girls and boys holding silver cups. She wondered whether she could ever be on a swimming team and win a cup.

Behind Falcon, Mr. Winter, the janitor, unlocked the pool-room door and went inside with his mop and bucket. He didn't notice that the door hadn't shut behind him.

Suddenly Falcon heard, "Look at me swim!" and a loud splash. She turned around fast, and ran into the pool room. Toody had jumped into the pool at the deep end, and she saw him sink beneath the surface as she ran. He bobbed up, thrashing frantically and choking, as she reached the pool. Then he disappeared. She dove underwater and saw him floundering. She grabbed for him, but his arm slithered out of her hand again and again. She needed to breathe; she couldn't see. Then her arms wrapped hard around something, and she shot to the surface. There were two splashes, and Frank and Mei were beside her, lifting Toody onto the edge of the pool. Tom grabbed him, laid him flat, and pushed the water out of him: gallons and gallons, it seemed to Falcon. She sat on the tile with Frank holding her and telling her she was a brave girl.

Toody sat up, looking surprised, and when he saw the scared faces around him, he started to cry. Mei Chu put her arms around him and held him tightly. She looked over the top of his head at Falcon and told her she was a brave girl. Her eyes were so kind, and Toody looked so small in her arms, that Falcon seemed to see him underwater again, and she began to cry too.

She cried and cried. She cried all the tears she had held in since her father had left and Toody had been born. She cried out the pool, the rain, the rivers, and all the oceans, with Frank and Tom patting her and saying, "It's okay, hon." Mei Chu had one arm around her, and one around Toody. He had stopped crying and was watching his sister. He had never seen her cry before, and it was very interesting to see how wide she could open her mouth.

Mei said they'd both had enough water for one day, and in no time at all they were dressed and in a cab, on their way back to West 77th Street.

All the way there Falcon tried to think of a way to keep Missy from finding out that she had let Toody almost drown. To her horror, when they reached number 16, Mei Chu got out of the cab with them.

"You don't have to come in. We're fine," said Falcon.

"It's time I met your mother, Falcon, and I have to tell her what happened," said Mei. There was nothing to do but follow her to the elevator.

Falcon let them into 4B with the key she wore on a string around her neck. The place was a mess. Empty take-out containers covered the coffee table. T-shirts and socks were draped over the furniture, sticky mugs and glasses stood on every surface, and the Sunday *New York Times* had spread itself everywhere. A vase of dead gladiolas stood on the piano, shedding dried petals onto the keys. The only tidy thing in the whole room was Henry, who was crouched neatly on a pizza box with his paws tucked under and his green eyes staring.

"I guess my mother's not home," said Falcon, "so maybe—"

"Hi, babes, how was Swim. Well, I made the deadline—let's go celebrate!" called Missy, walking into the living room. Falcon was glad to see that she had on a clean blue jumpsuit, and that her hair was freshly washed and combed. "How about . . . oh. Hi," said Missy.

Mei Chu introduced herself and told Missy what had happened at the pool. When she said that Toody might have drowned if Falcon hadn't rescued him, Missy's face turned greenish white and she sat down suddenly on the nearest chair. "Drowned?" she said, looking at Toody, who was eating a very gloopy peanut-butter sandwich, and teasing Henry with a catnip mouse.

Mei Chu sat down next to Missy and said she was so sorry and that Toody was fine, and Falcon was very brave. She patted Missy's arm gently, and told her what a good swimmer Falcon was, and how Toody wasn't afraid of the water anymore. Then she took a class schedule out of her pocket and explained about pool rules, and swim times. "You see," she said, "we can't supervise the children until class time, so it's best if the parents don't bring them before two forty-five."

"Oh sure, right," said Missy, still looking sick. "How could Toody drown? He can swim, can't he?"

Mei glanced at Falcon. She had sent Falcon home with notes about Toody several times. "Apparently, he thought he could. I'm sorry. I assumed you knew."

Missy looked confused. She got up, went over to Toody, knelt down, and put her arm around him. She told him he didn't have to go to Swim if he didn't want to, and that it was all right if he couldn't swim.

"I can so swim!" he roared. He shoved his mother away, leaving a blob of peanut butter on her sleeve. "I can do the crawl and the side and the breast," he shouted, demonstrating all three at once, nearly hitting his mother in the nose with his whirling elbows.

"Oh Lord, okay, okay! You can go!" said Missy, trying to get Toody to stop thrashing.

Mei stood up and said she was sorry again. She shook Missy's hand, and invited her to come see the class. Then she told Falcon and Toody she'd see them the next day, and left.

Missy locked the door after her, and looked at Falcon, who was trying to tidy the room. She had picked up all the empty food containers and stuffed them into a plastic shopping bag.

"Falcon, sit down," she said. Falcon set down the bag, walked over to the couch, and sat, not looking at her mother.

"How come you didn't tell me Toody can't swim?"

Falcon squirmed. "I thought you'd make us stop going to junior swim. Anyhow, he was getting better. He goes in the water now."

Missy began to lecture her about responsibility,

and being the oldest, but when she saw Falcon's eyes fill up at the word "drowned" she stopped, and held her. They sat like that for a while, until Falcon stopped sniffling.

"Emily says I should pay more attention to you," said Missy.

Falcon thought about that. She thought about Lily's family and all their rules.

"I'd like it if you could be the mother more," she said slowly. Missy's face got red.

"I'm sorry. I know you get stuck with Toody a lot. But next fall he'll be in school all day."

She ran her hands through her hair, stood up, and grinned down at her daughter.

"Come on, birdlet, you're a hero! Let's clear up and go out to dinner tonight: Kendo's. We'll sit on the floor."

Falcon got up and began shoving the dead gladiolas into the plastic bag. She wished her mother didn't think every problem could be fixed by going out to dinner.

Missy raced around the room piling socks, shoes, and T-shirts into a big bundle, dumped it in her bedroom, and shut the door.

She scrubbed a wet washcloth over Toody's sticky

face, and before he had time to protest, she said, "Let's go to Kendo's and eat till we pop!"

"Yay!" said Toody. He loved the Japanese restaurant. Mr. Kendo always made him a special red lacquer box of vegetable sushi, sweet-potato tempura, and beef on a skewer. They all liked sitting on the floor and eating with chopsticks, though Toody usually ended up using a spoon, or his fingers. Mr. Kendo said Falcon was the Davies Chopstick Champion. He always brought her a little dish of ice cubes at the end of the meal, and said, "You pick these up, you are the Super-Dooper Chopstick Champion!"

That night after they had finished eating, Toody and Missy sat cross-legged watching Falcon try to pick up an ice cube with her chopsticks. She held her breath and got a good grip on the smallest cube. But then she squeezed too hard, and the cube went flying, PLOP! right into Missy's teacup.

Mr. Kendo laughed. "No Super Dooper tonight!"

"Oh yes she is," said Missy, giving Falcon a hug. "Maybe not with chopsticks, but this is one Super-Dooper Champion Girl, for sure!"

"For sure!" agreed Mr. Kendo, and brought them all green-tea ice cream on the house.

CHAPTER EIGHT

*T*he next day they all slept late, and then Missy, in a sea-green dress and high-heeled shoes, bustled around, burning toast and slicing oranges. She was going to the bank to get money for paintbrushes, fancy paper, and tiny bottles of smell-of-the-week essences. Falcon hoped she wouldn't get patchouli, which always made Falcon choke.

"To the bank, to the bank, to the bank bank bank," sang Missy. "Falcon, my bird of birds, what are you doing today?"

"Taking Toody to Ardene Taylor's after Swim," she said.

"Well!" said Missy. Toody's mouth fell open and he stared at Falcon. Chewed-up toast and jelly ran down his chin, which for some reason made Falcon laugh.

Missy consulted the spiral notebook where she kept notes on everything from grocery lists to her secret smell-of-the-week formulas, and asked them what they wanted for dinner. They both voted for barbecue from Billy's on 89th Street.

"Red meat, fat, sugar, oh Lord. Well, all right, just this once. I'm gone." She opened the door. "Oh and don't forget, Swim at two forty-five sharp." The door slammed.

By the afternoon, when Falcon went to get Toody at his play group, it was starting to rain: big, fat, slow drops. Janny's mother gave them a ride to Swim. They had to run for it from the car, and were soaked before they reached the door of the old high school. It was 2:45 exactly by the clock behind Tom's desk.

Mei Chu gave them each a hug when they walked into the pool room and said, "Today, Mr. Tudor Davies, you are going to learn to tread water."

"Yay!" he yelled, and began windmilling his arms like mad.

To Falcon's surprise, Toody learned to tread water that day, without any fuss. Mei Chu held him around the middle in the shallow end, while he bicycled with his feet and sculled with his hands.

He kept on treading water after class, all the way

home in the cab, out onto the street, and into number 16.

Missy was still out, and there was a note stuck to the door. It said,

My dear Ms. Falcon,
  Sorry got tied up, back very late. Pizza for dinner there's money on my dresser and a treat.
  Love you little bird.
  Missy

Missy's dresser was littered with junk: odd earrings and broken necklaces, subway tokens, bills and postcards, overdue library books, glasses with flecks of orange stuck to their insides, a bottle of aspirin, an empty cassette case labeled "A Portrait of Patsy Kline," a crumpled red knee-high stocking, and a couple of dozen tiny bottles of essences: rose, lilac, cinnamon, musk, vanilla, oak moss. There was a cleared space in the middle, with a miniature bottle of vodka holding down a twenty-dollar bill. Next to it was a new, unopened box of After Eights.

Falcon looked at the postcards. One had a picture of a beach with a row of white hotels on it. It said "Having terrible time. Rain, flies, boredom. Please

Mags don't forget Mon. the 8th! Back Sun. nite, RC."
That was from Missy's agent. She was the only one
who called her Mags. The other postcard was from
Falcon's father. It had a picture of an airport, and no
stamp or postmark. It said, "How was Xmas? Hope
bratskies are fine, you too. Check enclosed. Love,
Peter." She looked in vain for the envelope, hoping
there might be more. The postcard picture was the
same as the one in her treasure box:

> *Dear Bird,*
>   *This is Sydney airport since you say you've*
> *enough koalas. Gorgeous no? I don't think.*
> *Glad you spent $ on NatHistMu membership*
> *instead of booze and wild parties. Here is butter-*
> *fly kiss.*
>   *Love,*
>   *Peter*

Falcon opened the After Eights, and took out two
of the waxy brown envelopes. She slipped out a thin
dark square, and took a bite that melted instantly
into a sweet sharpness on her tongue. It usually hurt
her feelings when Missy changed plans at the last
minute, but this time it suited her fine.

She went to her room and put the chocolates into her treasure box, next to the things Peter had sent her. Then she pulled out her favorite picture of her father. He wore an elaborate costume of leaves and feathers, and was dancing around a fire with a very old man in the same kind of costume. The dance was part of his training in South American folk medicine, and his face in the picture looked completely happy. Falcon stared at the picture for a long time, and then laid it carefully beside her seashells, her drinking gourd, and the nearly bald teddy bear that had belonged to her father when he was little.

She called Nino's Original Pizza, ordered a large with peppers, mushrooms, and sausage, and gave Toody the other envelope of chocolate. He stuffed it into his mouth whole. "Where's Missy?" he asked.

"Out. We're going to Ardene's, remember?"

The pizza came, and after they had eaten, Falcon wiped the tomato and chocolate smears off Toody's face and sat him down on the living-room sofa. She had decided to tell him about the Egg but she wanted to make sure that he understood about secrets, so he wouldn't tell Missy.

A year ago he had started a fire in Missy's bedroom. He poured three of her perfumes onto one of the roses on the rug, and made a neat pile of matches over the wet spot. Falcon came into the room just as he struck the last match on the box. As the matches flared up, she screamed, shoved him away, and dumped the Diet Pepsi she was carrying over the flames, which went out sizzling, leaving an awful stink behind. The rug had a large, black, sticky hole near its fringed edge. They spent the next hour dragging the rug around so that the hole would be hidden under Missy's bed, where she never vacuumed. That was the first time Toody had heard about secrets, and he had kept that one for a whole year.

Falcon sat close to Toody and opened her eyes wide. She spoke in her deepest, most serious voice, and told him all about finding the Egg. She said it was a secret like the rug, only magic. Lowering her voice to a scary whisper, she told him he must never ever tell anyone, not even Missy, about the Magic Egg. Toody wasn't sure what magic was, but he hated eggs.

"Do I have to eat it?" he asked suspiciously.

"No! You have to help guard it. You have to be a Friend of Egg."

"Okay," he said, cheerful now that there was no prospect of having to eat it.

Falcon pulled the big old leather-bound Bible out

of the bookcase, and set it on the coffee table. She pressed Toody's left hand on the Bible and told him to put his other hand on his heart, like the Pledge of Allegiance.

Toody put his hand on his stomach and stood proudly. "I pledga legions Tudor flag—" he began.

"No!" snapped Falcon. "Say, 'I swear on the Holy Holy Holy Bible to never say anything about the Magic Egg, cross my heart and hope to die!' "

"Swear the Holy Holy Eggs Magic, cross my heart and hope to die! Not even Missy," he added, for good measure.

Falcon put the Bible back on the shelf and led the way to the elevator and up to Ardene's. Just before she rang the bell, she said to him, "Remember, you swore."

"I know," he said solemnly, "cross my heart."

Ardene opened the door, and raised one eyebrow enquiringly when she saw Toody. "He knows it's a secret," said Falcon. "He swore on the Bible."

"I don't have to eat eggs," said Toody, just to make sure.

Ardene grinned and opened the door wide. Falcon led the way into the living room, where the fur hat sat right in the middle of the coffee table. Toody stared as Ardene pushed down the edge of the fur. There was the Egg, bright, reddish gold, and almost too hot to touch (127° Fahrenheit on Ardene's candy thermometer). Toody moved closer to the table, his eyes fastened on the Egg.

"Look but do not touch, Tudor," said Ardene. He put his hands behind his back.

"What is it?" he whispered.

"We don't know. We'll see when it hatches," said Falcon.

He could feel the heat on his face.

"What does it do?" he asked.

"It doesn't do anything, hon. It's growing inside, like the baby chicks at the zoo, and we hope it's going to hatch." Ardene had one hand on Toody's back. She thought he looked scared.

Toody knew that "hatch" meant the same as "born," and that being born was a great and important thing. He turned, ran toward the door, and tugged at the doorknob.

"I need to get my skin!" he said.

"What on earth does he mean?" asked Ardene.

"His snakeskin," said Falcon. "Peter brought it from Australia." She opened the door and followed him as he ran down the hall to the stairs. They came back up in the elevator because Toody had to hold the sandalwood box in both hands. Ardene and Falcon watched as Toody walked toward the table, holding the box out before him. He put it down near the edge and lifted the lid. The snakeskin was greenish brown, dull now that there was no live snake inside it to make it shine. It was five feet long, and very dry and thin, like the skin that peels off when you get a bad sunburn. It was Toody's most precious possession in all the world, and no one, not even Missy, was allowed to touch it. He pushed the box close to the hat with two fingers, till it was pressed against the dark fur.

"Here," he said. "This is for You. It's a present." They were all quiet for a minute, watching the glowing Egg.

"Well, Tudor," said Ardene, "you have made the First Gift. You are a true Friend of Egg." She pushed the thick, light brown hair off his forehead with the same look she sometimes gave Falcon, who had a sudden empty feeling in her stomach, in spite of all the pizza.

"It's just an old dead skin," she muttered. At that moment, the Egg moved. Only a tiny bit, but they all saw it. A little jiggle, a pause, then another jiggle.

Nobody breathed. Then there was a sound, a sound so faint, so brief that they weren't sure they had really heard it.

"Oh my goodness, I think it's going to hatch!" said Ardene.

CHAPTER NINE

*a*n hour later the Friends of Egg were gathered in Ardene Taylor's living room. Aunt Emily sat in a tall, curly armed velvet chair, like a throne. Freddy Maldonado sat cross-legged by the coffee table with his stethoscope, Ardene's candy thermometer, a shoebox lined with cotton, several small jars labeled "Reptile Food," "Wild-Bird Mixture," "Raptor Diet," "Desiccated Mealworm Blend," and "Vitaminized Hummingbird Nectar," an eyedropper, two of Ardene's oven mitts, a magnifying glass, a spiral notebook, three sharpened number 2 pencils, and a camera without any film in it. Toody and Falcon sat on either side of him, and Ardene sat on the center cushion of the brown sofa. Ardene had lifted the Egg in its napkin gently out of the hat and set it on the table.

They had been sitting for fifteen minutes, staring at the Egg, which had been silent and motionless the whole time. "Are you quite sure it moved, Ms. Taylor?" asked Aunt Emily.

"It moved. Twice."

"And squeaked," said Falcon.

"Well, I'm not positive it squeaked, but it did move," said Ardene, folding her arms and leaning back against the cushions.

"Shhh," said Freddy Maldonado. He had the bell of the stethoscope right against the Egg and was trying to hear. They all sat very still. Freddy sat up, his face flushed.

"Definitely. Something moving. Not just heartbeat. Tapping."

The Egg was perfectly still for a few more minutes, and then it jerked. A hairline crack appeared on the top. Nothing else happened for what seemed a very long time, and then the Egg really began to move. It quivered, tilted, and rolled over. The crack lengthened, widened, and a tiny beak emerged at the top. "Egg tooth," said Freddy hoarsely, staring with all his might.

There was another long pause. Suddenly a gush of steam burst out, and the Egg split into three pieces. There, curled tightly, lay a small, wet, weak-looking creature.

It rested for a few minutes in the largest piece of shell, and then it raised its head, thrust out a miniature claw, and crawled out of the shell onto the linen napkin. There was a smell like ironing. The little beast slowly uncoiled itself as they watched, and they saw that it was quite, quite perfect. It was about six inches long. ("Fifteen centimeters exactly," said Freddy, who measured it later.) A crest ran from the back of its head to the base of its long tail, which had a pointy end like an arrowhead. Its head was rather like a seahorse's, but its eyes were dark blue ("Just like a human baby," said Ardene, in awe) and were fringed with fine golden lashes and gold eyelids. It was red all over, lighter on the belly, which was round and rubbery. The skin on it back was faintly textured, with a regular pattern of half circles, and its feet had minute gold claws at the ends. It seemed to find its wings rather heavy, for they uncoiled last, with difficulty, and dragged behind like an oversize raincoat.

"What is it?" whispered Falcon.

"Dinosaur!" said Toody at the same time, staring with all his might.

"A lizard of some kind, though I've never . . ." said Freddy, staring.

"But it has wings," said Ardene. "It almost looks like a—"

"Oh my! Oh my!" said Aunt Emily, in such a strange voice that they all looked at her. Her face was very pale, and she was crying. "Oh don't you see?" she said. "It's a dragon!"

"Dragon! No such thing!" said Freddy.

"Of course there is, just look, and who would know better than I, oh the lovely, lovely thing. I wondered all along but I never . . ." She took out a handkerchief and wiped her eyes. "You, Freddy, may be an expert on birds, but I am an expert on dragons." Her face was shining with happiness.

Just then the little dragon, if that's what it was, tottered onto the tabletop. It crawled quite steadily for a few inches, then sat down suddenly and said, "GRAK!"

"Grak . . ." said Falcon softly.

"Grak?" the creature repeated, turning to look at her.

"Grak," said Falcon again. The hatchling crept toward her till it was only a few inches from the edge. She reached out cautiously. It watched her hand as it approached, and its blue eyes crossed as they tried to focus. Falcon's hand stopped an inch from its nose. The hatchling stretched its head forward, sniffed, and sneezed hard, knocking itself flat. "MMRRAAA!!" it wailed, and climbed onto Falcon's palm, its tail dangling over the side.

Falcon cradled it in her two hands, close to her chest. "Oh you beenie thing," she crooned, feeling its prickly claws and the warmth of its body against her skin.

"Does it burn?" asked Aunt Emily anxiously.

"Nnnoo," said Falcon, "he's warm but not hot. I think he's hungry."

"Yes yes. Now let's see," said Freddy Maldonado. "What will he eat?" He muttered to himself as he contemplated his assorted jars. Then he carefully poured some vitaminized hummingbird nectar into the cap of the jar, and put little piles of the other things onto the tabletop. "Here, try this," he said, filling the eyedropper with nectar and thrusting it at the creature, who squawked indignantly and bit him. "Hey!" he said.

"Let me," said Falcon. She dipped her finger in the nectar and held it out. A long blue tongue emerged and licked tentatively at the sweet drop. "I think he likes it," said Falcon, and offered more. It was enthusiastically lapped up, and so was a pinch of mealworm, a sticky glob of reptile food, and a gobbet of raptor diet. It turned the wild-bird seed over in its mouth with a dubious expression, and then spat it out "PHTOO!"

"How do you know it's a he?" said Ardene.

"A he?" said Freddy.

"You said 'he.' So did you, Falcon."

"It's the shape of the scales," said Aunt Emily. "That's how you tell the sex of dragons. Male dragons have triangular scales, females have semi-circular ones."

Freddy started to speak, then stopped. He was sure that Aunt Emily had lost her mind.

Falcon looked down at the little beast curled in her hands. It was trying to get the last drop of nectar off its nose with its blue tongue. Falcon set the dragon down on the napkin and ran a finger down its back.

"He doesn't, I mean, it doesn't have any scales," she said.

Aunt Emily leaned forward in her chair. "Look at those markings. I'm sure they will turn into scales later on. They're half circles. I think it's a girl!" she said triumphantly. "Though, of course, you can never be sure with dragons."

She sat back and asked Ardene for a glass of water. Emily took a long drink, and wiped her mouth with the back of her hand, which astonished Falcon more than anything else.

"I haven't lost my mind, Freddy, though I know you think I have," said Aunt Emily. She reached out to stroke the creature, oblivious to its heat. "Such a long time," she said. She looked up at them. They all waited, watching her.

"I've seen dragons before," she said, "a long time ago when I was young, during the Great War. I've told you, Falcon, about Charles, my fiancé whose plane was shot down over France.

"I was too sad to cry, or scream, or talk, or even eat. I just wandered the city, day after day, rain or shine. Everyone tried to help: our cook made delicious things to tempt me, my father offered to send me to Italy, my mother dosed me with castor oil, but nothing worked. I was sick with sadness. Finally Papa got fed up and forbade me to walk in the rain, or after sunset. So I began to sneak out late at night, when the household was asleep.

"One day, when I was sitting by the river, a man sat down beside me. He looked like a tramp, as we called them then. Now they are called the homeless.

They looked bad, and smelled bad, and people were afraid of them. But this one was different. His clothes had been washed so often that they looked silvery, and he smelled good. It was the smell that made me notice him because it made me think of rain and earth, and sheets drying in the sun on a windy day. There was something smoky too: tobacco or burning leaves, I thought, but it wasn't, it was hair, singed hair. I saw that his eyebrows had been curled crisp, and his hair stood out in a halo around his head as though he had faced a brief and sudden heat. His face was pink and shiny—I thought he'd been sunburned.

" 'Dragons,' he said. 'I teach dragons to dance.' I thought he was crazy, but then he smiled, and I wasn't afraid anymore.

" 'Dragons take a lot of teaching,' he said. 'So I'm always glad of a place to sit down. Dancers, waiters, mailmen: always happy to rest our feet.'

" 'Yes,' I said. 'Well, I must go now. It was nice chatting with you, Mr. Uh . . .'

" 'George,' he said. 'Just call me George.'

" 'And I am Emily,' I said, and stuck out my hand. He took it in his own for a moment, and smiled at me again. 'Good-bye then,' I said.

"I used to see him now and then, in the parks or by

the river, and I always felt better when I did. But I didn't want to feel better. So I held on to my sadness, and it got worse and worse.

"One drizzly April night, I walked all the way to Central Park. Even in those days, people didn't go there after dark, but I didn't care. I ran up the winding path. The rain was letting up, fog was rising from the grass, and I saw Belvedere Castle on my left. I walked around it, climbed the big rock, and sat down. Something was moving in the fog over the Great Lawn. I heard music and, suddenly, there was George in the moonlight, swaying, waving his arms, and calling out the measure, teaching the dragons to dance.

"Dragons! The fog, I saw, came from the heat of their breath, turning the wet air to steam as they pranced and leaped and turned. All sizes, and all ages too: young dragons the size of ponies, tumbling over their own feet; ancient dragons with skin hanging in folds, treading the ground a little behind the beat. All around the edge of the lawn were the great ones at the height of their power, sending tornadoes of steam into the sky. And at the back, blazing through the mist: the Seeing One, her wings rimmed with moonlight, blue flame flickering along her tail.

"George turned to face me and held out his hand. The music paused, and the dragons waited as I climbed down and put my hand into George's. He twirled and released me as the music began again, and I found myself dancing too. I danced till my skin glowed warm as dragonhide, waltzing, jigging, spinning." Aunt Emily, eyes half closed, swayed in her chair, remembering.

"Then," she said, "the Seeing One raised one great wing, and touched the lowest point of the moon. It tipped like a silver flagon and poured a shower of shining liquid onto the tongues of the thirsty dragons. 'Drink,' said George. 'Drink and dance, dance and drink,' and I turned my face up to feel cool drops on my skin, and tasted moonwine, mixed with tears. I drank and danced till I grew sleepy, then I curled up against the warm belly of an ancient dragon and went to sleep beneath her rough wings.

"When I woke it was almost dawn, and the Great Lawn was bone dry. My clothes were dry too, even my boots. I walked out of the park and took a bus home.

"After that, I wasn't afraid to be happy. I went to Italy, to China, Africa, and South America. I learned a great deal, and forgot even more. I kept on walking.

Now they say it is good for you: aerobic. I never saw George again. But I remember. When I first saw the Egg, I wondered, and now it's come true—this is a dragon!"

Aunt Emily took a deep breath, coming back from that April day three quarters of a century ago. She looked at the faces around her. Falcon sat on the floor with her arms around Toody. Freddy clutched a sofa cushion to his chest, and his eyes glistened. Ardene sat curled on the sofa, gazing into Aunt Emily's face. Aunt Emily smiled at her, at all of them.

"A dragon," she said again.

Freddy put down the pillow and touched the little creature with the tips of his fingers. "Of course," he said softly. "Of course."

"But dragons," said Ardene, "aren't they dangerous? The ones you saw weren't, but—"

"Oh but they were!" said Aunt Emily. "That was the point."

"Yes. Yes, of course. I see," said Ardene.

Falcon didn't see at all, but she said, "She's only little, she's a baby."

"Yes," said Freddy, "baby-alligator size, no problem for a while, infant, helpless."

The dragon had gone to sleep in the napkin. Falcon lifted it gently into the fur hat, where it lay curled with its tail over its nose, emitting rhythmic snorts of steam.

Toody, who had been staring, enchanted, at the dragon, said, "What's its name?"

Ardene gave him a hug. "That's a good question, Toody. What is her name?"

The grownups discussed this for some time, while the dragon slept. Freddy wanted a scientific Latin name. Aunt Emily, who had studied Ancient Greek, wanted to call her Derkesthai, which means "the Seeing One." She said that was where the word "dragon" came from. Ardene thought Falcon should pick the name, since she had found the Egg. They turned to her, sitting silent on the rug, with Toody beside her. He was watching the hat, from which small puffs of steam came at intervals. He picked up his snakeskin and draped it neatly over the dragon, who stirred and then snuggled more deeply into her dragon dreams. "Good night, Egg," he said softly.

"I don't think she should have a name—she's not a pet!" said Falcon fiercely, surprising everyone.

"She's right. The dragon is not a pet, and not tame. It's like a wild bird. A falcon, for instance," said Freddy. "When they are young and helpless, they seem tame because you can feed them and touch them. But they're not really; they'll always be wild."

"And she's Magic too," said Falcon. "She's not only wild, she's Magic."

So that's where they left it, and in the end they called the dragon Egg, as Toody had. "Which isn't a name," said Falcon, "it's just a . . ."

"Convenience," said Ardene.

CHAPTER TEN

*a*s time went on, the Friends of Egg found that the baby dragon would eat practically anything (except birdseed). After some thought, Freddy decided that a dragon was something like a hawk and something like an alligator. ("Not at ALL," said Aunt Emily scornfully, and Falcon agreed with her.) He worked out a diet of ground meat and fish, with some cod-liver oil and vitamins added. When they found the dragon devouring Ardene's African violets, Freddy decided that Egg needed some vegetables, so they tried lettuce and arugula and broccoli without success.

Finally, one day Ardene brought some edible flowers back from Balducci's: marigolds, nasturtiums, and elder and squash blossoms. She put a handful into the silver porringer that was the dragon's feeding dish. (It had "Emily" engraved on its side, and had belonged to Great-Great-Aunt Emily's great-grandmother.) The small creature sniffed, gave a joyful snort of steam, and gobbled up every blossom.

"I guess you liked that!" said Ardene, smiling at the dragon, whose nose was yellow with pollen.

"Grak! Grak!" said Egg.

The other problem was drink. Egg wouldn't touch the bowl of water they put down. Milk was no good either. ("Of course not. She's not a mammal," said Freddy Maldonado.) She did like to blow bubbles in the milk till it foamed up over the side of the dish.

"We could make cappuccino," said Falcon.

They were sitting around having tea: iced for Freddy, Falcon, and Ardene; apple juice in a teacup for Toody; and scalding-hot Earl Grey for Aunt Emily, who was never too warm. She had just poured it out when Egg, who was on the table as usual, stuck her whole head into the cup. Before they could move, the cup was half empty, and Egg was taking a breath before diving back in. "That was boiling hot!" said Ardene.

"Well, it makes sense," said Aunt Emily. "Maybe boiling water is what she needs."

Freddy Maldonado took notes. He had given up

trying to take pictures, even after he remembered to put film in his camera, because something always went wrong. Either he left the lens cap on, or he forgot to wind the film, or something. He had been brokenhearted when his shots of the hatching hadn't turned out (no film), so he decided to stick with notes and pencil sketches, which he did "Really beautifully," said Ardene, to make him feel better.

Ardene was right. His drawings, done quickly because Egg was seldom still, were full of life and very accurate.

From then on, Egg had a heavy pewter ashtray full of boiling water, set on a thick mat so as not to mark the table. It was a nuisance because she wouldn't touch the water if it cooled off. ("Not below one hundred and ninety-two degrees Fahrenheit," said Freddy, after conducting several experiments.)

By the beginning of August, Egg had grown almost two inches. Her eyes had changed to a clear blue-green, and looking into them was like slipping into deep, cool water. They were the only cool thing about her. Her glossy skin was noticeably hotter. They could still touch her, but they couldn't hold her for long without wearing gloves. The lining of the hat was marked with a dragon-shaped scorch. This was worrisome.

"How hot is she going to get?" asked Ardene. "You slept cuddled up to a dragon, didn't you, Emily? How hot was that?"

"That was an old, old dragon," said Aunt Emily, "They cool off in old age, just as I have. I could never have touched one of the great ones, or even the teenage dragons. They were hot enough to burn you up in a minute."

Egg sat on a heatproof pad on the table, stretching her wings, which no longer dragged behind her as she walked. She was beginning to make little hopping movements with her wings extended, though she hadn't left the ground yet. "When she does," said Ardene, "we'll have a problem."

"Why?" said Falcon. "Egg is sweet. She's not dangerous."

"She's dangerous if you forget that she's a dragon," said Aunt Emily gently.

"She's not, she is NOT!" said Falcon, jumping up and startling everyone, including Egg, who sailed off the table, wings spread wide. She landed, with a surprised look and a wobble, on the arm of the pink chair where Aunt Emily was sitting.

"She can fly!" said Falcon, stroking Egg's sea-horse head with a cautious fingertip. "You can fly!"

"She certainly can," said Ardene, grimly. There was

a scorching smell, and she quickly slipped a pot-holder under the little dragon's bottom.

Aunt Emily looked at the dragon next to her and at Falcon, who was gazing rapturously at Egg and crooning, "That was really good, that was just fine, you really flew, you sure did, you did."

"FAK! FAK!" said Egg, flapping her wings.

"Falcon," said Aunt Emily, "Falcon."

Falcon tore her eyes away from Egg and said, "Yes? What?"

"Falcon, she's going to grow much bigger and hotter."

"She doesn't mean to scorch things," said Falcon.

"Of course not," said Aunt Emily, "but a dragon is a dragon."

"The point is," said Ardene, "she can't stay here much longer. She'll start a fire."

There was a long silence while everyone's brain whirred and hummed. Finally Freddy suggested the aviary on the museum roof above his apartment. It had a garden, and a high wall, and no one else ever went up there. And it was covered with wire netting.

"What about the birds?" asked Ardene. "Won't Egg scorch them, or even eat them?"

"There aren't any birds there now," said Freddy, before Falcon had time to protest. "I only keep injured birds there, before re-introducing them to the wild. It's empty now. Well, except for my duck, Rothschild. He was hit by a car and his wing was so badly broken that he can never fly again. He lives in a nest in my office filing cabinet most of the time. The aviary would be perfect for Egg."

Falcon felt as though the grownups were galloping along, dragging her behind them. They were taking over even though she was the one who had found Egg in the first place. "How will I see her?" she asked. Her voice sounded squeaky and young.

"My apartment and office are two floors below, Falcon. You can see her anytime you like," said Freddy.

Ardene called for a vote, and they all agreed, except Falcon, who wanted time to think.

"While you're thinking, Egg will be scorching my furniture," said Ardene. "Look, why don't we move Egg just for the time being? Then, when you think of something better, we'll do that, hmm?"

"Well . . . I guess so," said Falcon.

CHAPTER ELEVEN

$\mathcal{T}$hey made the move that very night. Freddy carried the hat, with the dragon in it, across the street in an old leather satchel. They all went up in the creaky elevator together, and stepped out onto the tower roof.

Falcon didn't like the way the grownups were being so bossy, but she had to admit (to herself) that the southeast tower was a wonderful home for Egg. It was like an old castle, with tall battlements all around, and narrow slits for shooting arrows through. Stout wire netting stretched high over the roof. Small fruit trees grew in tubs around flower beds planted with marigolds, pansies, and impatiens surrounded with small polished stones. A concrete birdbath stood near a pile of sand, and there were several steel milk crates for sitting on. Beside the elevator a staircase spiraled down all six stories. A big plastic garbage can held a fifty-pound bag of wild-bird seed. Freddy usually forgot to put the lid on, and a family of mice had been feasting there for weeks.

It was a fine place to be, a secret, special place. The high walls kept out most of the city noise, and when Falcon looked up, she could see nothing but sky and birds. If she peeked through the notches in the wall ("Crenelations in the battlements," said Ardene), she could see into the topmost tree branches, and watch the people far below, knowing that they could not see her, and wondering what they would say if they knew she were there with a dragon of her very own.

Egg seemed to like her new home. There were flowers to munch, warm stones to bask on, sand to roll in, and plenty of room for the short flights she made. Falcon loved sitting on a milk crate, high above the city, watching Egg.

All the Friends of Egg liked to be there. Freddy brought a big old armchair up for Aunt Emily, where she sat with her feet propped on a milk crate, telling tales of New York in the Olden Days. Freddy's mallard duck, Rothschild, had taken a liking to her and sat in her lap, preening his beautiful brown and violet-blue feathers, and making duckish remarks.

The first time he saw Egg, he puffed himself up to twice his size, flapped his good wing, and squawked rude things at her in Mallardese. It scared her considerably, so she was careful to avoid him from then on.

Ardene, who took yoga classes four times a week, and was very limber, liked to sit on the floor, cross-legged. She usually prepared the little dragon's food because, as she said herself, "I am really a very good cook, even for dragons!"

Toody helped Freddy with the plants; he loved putting his hands into dirt.

"What's those?" he asked Freddy one day. Freddy had an old coffee can full of soft gray coils that looked like very long cigarette ashes. He was mixing them with potting soil and putting the mixture into big clay pots.

Freddy glanced at Ardene and Aunt Emily and turned very red. "I'll tell you later," he whispered.

"I want to know now," said Toody, reaching out a finger to touch the coils.

"Yes," said Emily, who had noticed them too. "What are they, Freddy? You haven't taken up smoking again, have you, after seven years without? Really,

Freddy, it seems very foolish, after all the trouble it was to quit, and you know how much better you feel since you stopped. I was so proud, I know it was hard for you. It seems a shame to begin again, and smell so dreadful, like a dirty ashtray, and all those burn holes in your clothes, I do think—"

"They're TURDS!" Freddy blurted desperately.

"What did you say?!?" said Aunt Emily. Falcon, who was playing with Egg, looked up, and Ardene burst out laughing.

Freddy's face was now absolutely scarlet with embarrassment. "I'm sorry, Emily, but I'm not smoking, and that's what they are. Turds, dragon excrement, from Egg. They're made of ash; I kept finding them and not knowing what they were, until I saw her one day after her breakfast. She was squatting down with that sort of . . . concentrated look that cats get when they're in their litter pan, and that's what she . . . produced. I analyzed them; they're full of minerals; they make the most superb fertilizer. Just look at my marigolds!"

Ardene and Falcon were helpless with laughter. Toody touched an ashy gray coil with his finger and looked puzzled. And now Aunt Emily's face was red. "Well!" she said.

"What are those, I said. I want to know!" said Toody.

"It's doo-doo," said Falcon. "It's dragon poop. It's Egg's number two," she said, sending herself into another fit of laughter.

"Does Egg need diapers?" asked Toody.

Freddy grinned. "I don't think you can diaper a dragon," he said. "Anyhow, it's good for the flowers."

By mid-August, the dragon's beloved fur hat was a tight fit and smelled of burned hair. When they put Egg into the nice fireproof box Freddy had fixed, she clambered right out again and squeezed herself back into the hat.

"I know!" said Aunt Emily. "Falcon, fetch my bag, would you?" She took out a pair of small scissors shaped like a stork with a long, sharp beak, and snipped the threads that held the seams of the hat together. Egg watched anxiously, making little worried noises.

The hat, its seams undone, opened out into a four-petaled flat shape, like a big brown flower. As Aunt Emily set it into the box, something bright jingled onto the floor.

"Oh look!" said Falcon, picking it up. "Treasure!"

"Why it's my garnet necklace!" said Ardene.

Aunt Emily was feeling in the scorched lining of the hat. "Are these yours too?" she asked, holding out her hand. A topaz brooch and several rings with colored stones sparkled in her palm.

Freddy laughed. "Just like the Corvidae," he said. "Crows, magpies. Like to steal shiny things."

"No," said Aunt Emily, "not like a crow, like a dragon. Dragons love treasure, not to steal, but to guard. Egg was guarding your treasure, Ardene."

"But how could she have known where they were?" said Ardene. "I keep them in a locked case in the back of the topmost shelf of my closet. I hardly ever wear them."

"Dragons know," said Aunt Emily, letting the handful of gems and gold fall back into the scorched remains of the hat. Egg shoved her nose under the jewelry, pushing it into a neat pile. "Merkle, merkle, merkle," she muttered. Then she half hopped, half flew into the box, turned around three times, and settled happily onto the glittering heap.

"Magic!" said Falcon, scratching Egg under the chin in the way she loved. The little dragon's sparkling eyes were half closed in ecstasy.

"Dragon Magic," said Aunt Emily.

CHAPTER TWELVE

$\mathcal{F}$alcon began to spend more and more time on the tower roof, watching Egg's brief flights with a vaguely uneasy feeling. Each day the dragon flew a little closer to the wire netting that hung overhead. Each day her wings wobbled less. When the other Friends of Egg came up, they exclaimed over Egg's progress and growth. Falcon thought they sounded like a bunch of stupid cooing pigeons.

On August 31st Falcon was on the tower roof with Freddy and Egg. There was a full moon: an end-of-summer moon, low, fat, and orange.

It was after eleven o'clock, and Falcon had snuck out of the apartment after Missy and Toody were asleep. Freddy, who didn't know much about children, asked her whether it was all right for her to be out.

"Oh yes," she said. "Missy says I am very mature for my age."

Egg arched her wings, like a dancer doing stretches at the barre, and looked up at the moon. It seemed to hang just out of reach above the wall of the tower. As Freddy and Falcon watched, she stood on the very tips of her talons, rose into the air, and sailed smoothly once around their heads. Around she went again, higher still, until her wings grazed the netting, sending a shower of sparks down onto the roof. Falcon cried out as one of them touched her face just above the left eye. The sudden sting made her eyes fill with tears, and in a blur she saw the little dragon land beside the electric kettle of scalding water that had replaced the pewter ashtray.

Egg took a long drink, and belched out a cloud of steam that enveloped her head before blowing away.

"Are you all right?" asked Freddy.

"Yes, just a spark," said Falcon in a slightly strangled voice. Freddy took her hand away from her face, and saw a red mark the size and shape of a lentil.

"Ice," he said, and disappeared through the doorway that led to the steps of the tower. He came back with a bowl of ice cubes. "There," he said, wrapping a piece of ice in his handkerchief, and dabbing it on her head. She winced—the ice was dripping down her neck, but it did take the sting away. "It's going to blister," he said, peering closer in the bright moonlight. "You may have a scar."

"I don't care," she said, watching Egg, who was eating the last bits of Ardene's dragon-food mixture from her silver porringer. "She touched the wire."

"She's growing fast," said Freddy. "Soon we'll have to let her go."

Falcon shouted "NO!" startling him, and knocking the bowl of ice to the floor.

"What the . . . ?" he said indignantly. "What's wrong with you anyhow?"

"Can't you see? She'll go away and never come back, and she'll probably die. We can't let her go. She's mine. I found her."

"Nobody owns a dragon, Falcon," Freddy said quietly.

Falcon glared at him. "What do you know? You all think you know everything. You'll see!" She stormed out the tower door.

Freddy sighed, picked up the bowl, and looked at Egg, who was chasing an ice cube across the floor.

When she touched it with her nose, it vanished in a puff of steam. "More dinner?" he said, and went to get it. The dragon stretched her wings and craned her long neck to look up at the moon. She gave a low, drawn-out call, and all the sounds of the city were suddenly still.

CHAPTER THIRTEEN

*I*n September, New Yorkers don't know whether it's summer or fall. Sometimes the August heat lingers, damp and heavy, and people drag themselves around from one air-conditioned place to another, short-tempered and sweaty. Then, one morning they wake up and wish they had a blanket on the bed. The sky is blazing blue and there's a fine strong wind that carries a promise of roasted chestnuts and wood smoke. In the parks the leaves begin to fall, golden yellow, and the wind picks them up and sends them dancing above the sidewalks.

Falcon woke each morning with a sick feeling in her stomach, for school had begun again. She had hoped that this year would be better. She was in the "A" group with Ms. Serkorian. Ms. Serkorian had a round, happy face, and she encouraged outside reading. She brought in copies of *The Last Dodo,* and told the class that Falcon's mother had painted the picture on the jacket. Everyone stared. Linny Kressler said, "Falcon is soooo special" under her breath and the boys in the back made bird noises. Falcon kept her eyes on the book in front of her, and wished she could just leave, as she had in first grade. Lily Weng was in Ms. Serkorian's class too, but she hung out with Penny Alden and Linny now. They clustered together at recess, whispering and giggling at the swaggering boys.

One thing *was* better. Toody had started kindergarten, and was having a wonderful time. When the other children laughed at him and called him Doody he laughed too, and announced to his teacher that his name was Doody Davies. It made him an instant hero to his classmates. The van brought him home after school, so Falcon had more time to herself. She spent all of it in the tower, watching the dragon.

The burn over her eye blistered, then scabbed over and itched like mad. She swabbed it with calamine lotion, and told her mother it was a bee sting. Two weeks after the night in the tower, Falcon took her saved-up allowance and went to a pet store on West 74th Street. She bought a chain collar and a retractable chain leash. She had a feeling the other Friends of Egg might not like the leash idea, so after school she went up to the tower by herself. She stuck her head into Freddy's office and asked him for the keys.

Freddy was sitting at his computer terminal. He and the computer were having a disagreement over the spelling of "Trochilidae".

He muttered, "On the chair by the door. Sure it's an 'a.' " The computer beeped back. "Oh, shut up."

Falcon climbed the stairs and unlocked the door to the roof. The dragon grakked and whistled when she saw her, and Egg galloped over to her porringer. Falcon filled it with chopped meat and mashed sardines. While the dragon was eating, Falcon put the collar and leash around Egg's neck, working quickly so as not to burn her hands. The dragon's wings were her hottest parts, but even her neck was almost too hot to touch.

Egg looked up, astonished, when she felt the collar, and craned her head around to look at the leash. She tried to see the cold thing she felt around her throat, but she couldn't. "Garg garg," she said sadly, and clawed at it with her foot.

"It's okay, Egg. It's a nice shiny collar. Now we can go for walks and you won't get lost." Egg shook her head hard, but the steel links around her neck didn't budge. She walked away from her dish, arched her wings, and rose into the air. The leash uncoiled as she flew, and she felt only a slight pull from its weight. Falcon stood in the center of the tower roof with the dragon flying in circles around her.

"Oh, Falcon!" said a voice behind her, and she turned to see Ardene and Freddy, with Toody in tow, in the doorway. Ardene's voice was full of sorrow. The dragon made one more circle and landed in the sand pile. The weight of the chain upset her balance, and she had to scramble to stand up.

Toody looked puzzled at the collar and leash.

"Was Egg bad?" he said.

"No, Egg wasn't bad," said Falcon. "It's a present. To keep her safe. See, she likes it, and we can take her for walks."

Ardene stared at her. "For walks? Where exactly, and when?"

"Well, at night, you know, around, when it's dark." Freddy hunkered down beside the dragon and examined the collar and leash. Egg liked the sound the leash made. She jerked her head rhythmically to make the chain go "thrink thrink thrink" on the stone floor.

Ardene looked up at the wire netting over the roof, and then down at the dragon. "If anyone else finds out about Egg, she'll be put into a zoo."

"Or worse," said Freddy. "Scientific research, specimen. Experiments, dangerous animal, stuffed and mounted probably."

In her mind, Falcon saw Egg stuffed, in a glass case like the animals in the museum. Her eyes filled with tears. "The leash will keep her safe," she said. "She can fly up here. Nobody will know." Her throat felt thick, and she was afraid she would cry.

Freddy scratched the top of the dragon's head with the fingernail he kept long for that purpose. "Endangered species," he said.

"That's true, Falcon," said Ardene. "She might be the only one."

"Aunt Emily saw lots of them," Falcon said. "Remember, she said there were lots, all sizes."

"Yes, well. I don't know, that was a long time ago. The world is very different now." Ardene put her arm around Falcon. "Why don't you talk to Emily? She knows more about dragons than anyone else."

Ardene's arm felt so good that Falcon longed to lean against her, but the thick, hot feeling filled her throat again, and she pulled away.

"Maybe she does and maybe she doesn't." She unhooked the leash from Egg's collar, and retracted it into the handle. Then she stalked out the door and marched down all six flights of stairs.

CHAPTER FOURTEEN

*T*hat night Falcon went to bed at 8, and set her clock-radio alarm for 2 a.m.

She woke up at four minutes to two, before the alarm went off, pulled on jeans and a navy-blue sweatshirt, and tiptoed to the door with her sneakers in her hands. The keys to the tower were in her pocket along with the pencil flashlight Peter had given her for Christmas. She had had the keys copied that afternoon. Her conscience told her it was a kind of stealing, but she refused to listen.

Falcon had thought hard about how to get by Enrico, the late-night doorman. Now she walked down the fire stairs to the basement, past the washer-dryers, and let herself out the door with the red EXIT sign over it. It locked behind her automatically and she sat down in the stairwell to put her sneakers on. She would have to stay out until 8 a.m. when Eddie, the daytime doorman, came on duty.

There was no one around when she emerged from the alley between number 14 and number 16. Cars went by occasionally on Central Park West, but 77th Street was quiet. The sky was overcast, not even the stars were out, and the city seemed big and dark. Falcon ran across 77th, and over the grass to the foot of the southeast tower. The museum loomed above her. She couldn't see any lights in the tower at all, though there were a few on elsewhere in the building.

She used the flashlight to light the keyhole so she could unlock the door. It opened slowly as she pushed. She took a deep breath, and began to climb, the thin beam of light at her feet cutting through the darkness.

She reached the top, and stood for a moment, catching her breath. Then she unlocked the roof door and stepped into the netted enclosure. Egg raised her head at the sound of Falcon's footsteps and said, "Grak?"

"It's me, Egg. We're going for a walk." Falcon snapped the leash onto Egg's collar, put on a pair of oven mitts, and carried Egg down the six flights of stairs. She looked carefully to make sure there was no one around, and moved quickly onto 77th Street toward Central Park West.

"Grak, grak, grak!" said the dragon.

"Shhh," Falcon said, and dashed across the street and into the silent park. She ran, Egg jouncing hotly against her chest, and emitting joyous puffs of steam scented with cod-liver oil. (Freddy always gave her her vitamins at dinnertime.)

Falcon came to a stop in a grassy, wooded space well inside the borders of the park, and set Egg down on the ground. "Mrrff!" said the dragon, and gazed around at this strange new place.

The shadowy trees rose all about them. The moonless night arched overhead. Frogs and crickets sang in the stillness, and the early fall air brought the scent of earth and grass, dead leaves and rain to the nose of the little dragon. She raised her head and breathed deeply. Then she gave the low dragon call that Falcon heard for the first time, and rose on glowing wings into the answering silence of the night. Up she went, the chain uncoiling from Falcon's outstretched hand. But the sky was very big and there was no moonlight. Suddenly Egg turned, and glided back down to land near Falcon's feet. "Foomk foomk!" she said in relief, and rubbed her chin against Falcon's shoe for reassurance.

She made only one more short flight that night, but they walked together through the park, slowly, stopping to examine every bush and stone. They saw raccoons and woodchucks, squirrels, and rats too, which made Falcon shudder. The dragon greeted them all with puffs of steam, and loud graks that sent the animals scurrying for safety. They walked halfway around the lake, waking the sleeping ducks, who squawked and flapped indignantly into the water, where the dragon would not follow. "Gurrrk?" she said sadly. She wanted to play.

At four o'clock Falcon picked the dragon up and made her way back to the museum. This time Egg made no noise at all. She was so tired that when Falcon set her down on the sand pile she grunted, tucked her tail over her nose, and fell asleep.

As Falcon crept down the tower stairs, she heard birds calling, and smelled the change in the air that meant dawn was coming. She ran across the street, slipped into the alley, and crouched uncomfortably on the stairwell behind the exit door, listening to the city wake up. Garbage trucks crashed and clattered, cars roared and honked. At eight o'clock she got up and ran through the alley to the front door of number 16, where Eddie was standing with a cardboard cup of coffee and a bag of jelly doughnuts, munching and enjoying the bright September day. Falcon ran past him shouting, "Morning!" making him spill his coffee.

"What the . . . ?" he said. "Hey! Where'd you come from?"

"Jogging," she said, as the elevator doors closed.

She made it back to 4B without seeing anyone but Mr. Mott, who lived in 4A. He was hidden behind the *Wall Street Journal,* and never noticed her.

Her mother was still asleep when she got in, but Toody was eating gingersnaps and watching *The Today Show.* "Where did you go?" he said.

"Out," she said.

"Out where?"

"Where where I don't care, here there everywhere," she chanted, snatching the box of gingersnaps.

"NO!" he roared, and chased her as she danced around, holding the box just over his head.

"I'm going to make coffee," she told him, and gave him back the cookies before he started to howl.

"With bubbles?" he asked.

"Yes," said Falcon, pouring milk into a saucepan to

boil, so it would foam up. She put two heaping tea-spoonfuls of coffee into her kangaroo mug, a half teaspoonful into Toody's koala mug, and poured in the hot milk, stirring hard to make a froth. "Sugar or honey?" she said.

"Honey honey honey!" sang Toody, who liked to squeeze the plastic bear.

Her own cup tasted very bitter in spite of the honey. She hoped it would wake her up. Her eyelids felt thick and gritty, and the strong coffee sloshing around in her stomach made her feel queasy. She wondered whether she might be sick, and put her hand to her forehead. She thought it was a bit hot.

"I'm sick," she said to Toody.

"No you're not," he said, peering at her. "Your face looks nice and fat."

"It's swollen—I probably have mumps. I'm sure I have a temp."

"Get the mometer!" said Toody, climbing on a chair to feel her head. He pressed his sticky palm against her face and they both waited for a minute. "Well, it's sort of hot," he said, "and your scab is coming off. Can I pick it?"

"No!" she said. "You are gross. Anyhow, I'm going to stay home from school."

"You can't. Missy'll be mad."

"No she won't. I'm sick, my tongue is gluey."

"Let me see." Falcon stuck her tongue out as far as it would go. Toody prodded it with a forefinger. "It's brown on top," he said.

She went to the hall mirror to look. Her tongue was brownish, and had pasty stuff in the middle. She thought it was mumps, for sure. She looked at the clock. It was only 8:34, which was too early to wake Missy, but she had to.

Only her mother's left hand and a bit of tangled hair were visible sticking out from under the comforter. Her hand was square with perfect oval nails, except for the left thumb. That was her chewing finger, and it was raggedy looking with a sore place on the side.

Falcon poked at the mound where she guessed her mother's shoulder was. There was a grunt from the comforter but no movement. "Missy, I don't feel good." Her mother's face emerged looking pink and crumpled.

"What? What is it, bird?"

"I'm sick. I have a stomach ache, I think I'm going to throw up, and I think I have a temp."

Falcon leaned over so her mother could feel her head. "Well. Sort of warmish. Did you take it?"

"No, but my tongue has brown gunk on it, see?"

"Oh God, no," said her mother, rolling over and pulling the comforter back up. "Please, don't, baby, hmm? Just get Toody off to school, would you, then you can take a children's Tylenol, and I'll make us some peppermint tea. Thanks, birdlet." Missy disappeared again.

By midmorning Falcon was groggy with sleep in spite of the coffee she had swallowed for breakfast. She wasn't sure if the queasy feeling inside was from that or from being too hungry. She started to eat a gingersnap, but it tasted terrible. At ten her mother got up, felt Falcon's head again, and made peppermint tea and cheese toast for both of them.

The toast was yummy and it was nice to sit alone with Missy, talking and sipping tea. It was almost like the time when she was little, before Toody was born, before the shouting began. Her father called them "The Forever-and-Ever Family," and there were no secrets. Falcon wished she could tell her mother about Egg. Missy loved tales about elves and trolls, magicians and dragons. And here was Falcon right in the middle of magic, and she couldn't say anything. She knew that if she told Missy about walking in the park at night, it would all be over. All the grownups would gang up and make her put Egg in a zoo, and then she wouldn't have anything. She would just be herself, fitting in nowhere, without friends or magic. She wondered if the children in the fairy tales ever felt the way she did, and she sighed.

"What's wrong, birdlet?" asked her mother.

"I wish I weren't me," she said.

Missy looked at her daughter. Then she poured out the last of the peppermint tea and gave Falcon a hug. "I'm glad you are you," she said. "You are very special." She kissed her on the head, picked up her mug, and went into the bedroom.

Falcon didn't feel special. "Special" meant popular like Lily, or pretty like Penny Alden. She pulled a strand of her hair over her face so she could see it. It was boring hair, she thought, not like Penny's bright coppery curls or Lily's shiny black braids. She wished she were a snake so she could shed her old skin and come out all beautiful and new.

Falcon thought about the way Ardene and Freddy had looked when they saw the chain on Egg, and how they had stared at her while she stood alone in the middle of the roof. She could feel the tower keys poking her through her pocket. They seemed to take up a lot of room, as though they carried all the bulk of her lies and secrets. She put her head down on the table between her outstretched arms, and shut her eyes.

CHAPTER FIFTEEN

*A*ll through that fall, Falcon took Egg out to the park whenever she could. Late Friday or Saturday nights were best because she could go back to bed afterward. But sometimes she went out during the week too. She told herself that it was for the dragon's sake. Mei Chu said you should work out at least three times a week, which was probably good for dragons too. The truth was that she loved the walks in spite of having to keep them secret. At night the park seemed full of magic.

Egg was growing stronger and less fearful of the empty sky. She rose easily now, arching her wings, letting the air currents lift her as she pushed against them, the muscles flexing under her shiny red skin. Her skin was changing too, the semicircles becoming more defined. If you ran your fingertips over her back, you could feel the pattern of half-moon scales. A beautiful green haze ran from her nose down her crest to her arrowhead-tail tip, and she was glossy all over like the tiny frogs in the Central Park Zoo. Egg wasn't tiny, though. She was the size of a beagle, and it was a chore to carry her down the tower steps and across the street to the park. In spite of the oven mitts, Falcon had a small burn on her wrist.

Ms. Serkorian asked her if she was getting enough sleep. Falcon liked her teacher, but she didn't want her snooping around or writing notes to Missy.

"Oh yes. I'm always tired in the fall," she said, to get away from that black-eyed stare.

That day Ms. Serkorian gave the class a lecture about eight hours of sleep a night, regular bedtimes, and not drinking things with caffeine in them.

After that, she started going to bed even earlier, right after supper.

"Are you all right, babe?" asked Missy.

"I think I'm growing," said Falcon. "It makes me sleepy."

By November 1st the park was very cold at night. Falcon wore a turtleneck, two sweatshirts, her down jacket, and her father's blue-wool watch cap. The oven mitts on her hands were badly scorched. Over her head, at the end of the leash, the dragon circled and soared, pulling Falcon's arm so hard it ached. She had to dig in her heels and flex her knees to keep from being lifted off her feet. The chain was wrapped several times around her arm, and she held on tightly with both hands.

"Egg!" she called into the sky. "Egg! Home!" Her voice sounded thin and small in the darkness, and the dragon circled, straining to fly toward the moon that hung over the distant lake.

Finally, just when Falcon was sure her arms would be pulled clean out of their sockets, Egg spiraled down and landed, with only a slight bump, at her feet. Egg was perfect at takeoff, but her balance on landing was still uncertain. Sometimes she landed beautifully and then just fell over, looking indignant. Now she gazed up at Falcon and said, "Gronk!" rubbing affectionately against her legs.

"That was good, huh, Egg?" said Falcon. She tugged gently on the leash. "Let's go home."

The dragon waddled along beside her, toward Central Park West. She was almost too heavy to lift now, and uncomfortably hot. But Egg seemed to accept the necessity of leaving the park and going back to the tower. She didn't like the stairs, though. Her fat, snaky body got tangled around itself on the spiral steps. Falcon was beginning to wonder whether she could use the elevator without waking Freddy, but it was old and creaky. She didn't quite dare. So she held a piece of beef jerky in front of the dragon's nose. "Mrph!" said Egg enthusiastically, and galumphed up the last flight. Falcon gave her the jerky and left her chewing away, her sides steaming gently in the pre-dawn air.

CHAPTER SIXTEEN

*a*utumn was over, and it was winter in New York City. The skies were gray with chilly patches of pale blue, and the wind that came around the corners of buildings caught you and found its way right through the wool jacket you thought would be warm enough. It was time for down coats, and hats pulled down to the eyebrows. In New York City people walked faster, shoulders high, breath puffing out through the gap between their scarves and hats.

When Falcon took Egg to the park, she had to jog in place under the flying dragon to stay warm. It was awkward because the pulling chain stretched her arms straight over her head, and it was hard to keep her balance. Her shoulders ached all the time and her body buzzed with sleepiness. Missy looked worried and made her take vitamins. She got Mrs. Frank in to watch Toody several times a week, and brewed herbal teas that tasted like boiled grass. "You look peaked, bird. If you're not better by Christmas, we'll go see Dr. Kahlmorgan. Maybe you're anemic." Falcon insisted she was fine, and obediently swallowed the pills and the tea. She was glad about Mrs. Frank. It meant she had more time alone with Egg.

On the Friday after Thanksgiving, she was sitting on the tower roof with Freddy and Aunt Emily, watching Egg. They all had taken off their coats, even Emily. The dragon gave off so much heat that they were warm and rather sleepy. Their coats, hats, mittens, and scarves were piled in a corner, forming a nest for Rothschild, who had had his own Thanksgiving dinner of mince pie and cranberries. Egg was taking a nap after eating a huge meal of Thanksgiving leftovers. She gobbled up the turkey and stuffing and gravy, and the mince pie, but when she took a mouthful of cranberry sauce she looked surprised, and hissed out a cloud of bright pink steam. Now she was lying in her sand bed, curled up, her jeweled eyes half closed. The green haze down her back had gone as far as it would go, and where it blended into the red, the scales were edged with gold. Her baby fat was beginning to smooth out, and her skin caught the light so that she sparkled as she breathed.

Rothschild stirred in his nest. He could smell the fresh, cold winter air blowing over the tower, even through the warmth of dragon heat. Maybe it reminded him of his wild-duck days, of flying over the park, and diving in the lake for delicious morsels of tadpole and water beetle. He got up, waddled toward the wall, and hopped up on the birdseed bin to have a look around. He never saw the dragon's eyes open or heard her wings, only felt the rush of heat as she seared him with her flaming breath. His cry of agony startled everyone out of their sleepiness, but they were too late. There was nothing left but a smoldering heap of feathers that had once been a duck.

As they watched in horror, the dragon nosed at the poor scorched corpse, picked it up in her jaws, and bit down. They heard an awful sound of crunching bones. She swallowed. "Grak!" she said happily.

"She killed him!" cried Falcon, through chattering teeth. "She burned him. Oh Rothschild! She ate him! I heard him scream!"

Aunt Emily wrapped her arms around Falcon. Her face was white and she was too shocked to speak. The dragon looked up at them and curled her long blue tongue out to get the last delicious taste of roast duck off her lips. Then she flew back to her sand bed and snuggled down. The gold lids over her eyes drooped, and closed.

Freddy bent down and picked up a single metallic-blue feather. He mopped at his eyes with a paper napkin and took a deep, shaky breath.

"She's a predator, Falcon," he said. "It's her nature to kill and eat things, like a hawk, or like Henry, for that matter."

"Henry only ever kills bugs. Anyway, Egg is different. She's special, she's Magic."

"She is. But she eats meat. Like us." He gulped. "Like the turkey." He knew he would never eat meat again.

"That's different! We didn't kill it. It didn't have a face!"

"Is it?" asked Freddy. "Somebody killed it. It used to have a face. Is that so different?"

"It is different. Aunt Emily was right; she is dangerous," cried Falcon.

Aunt Emily sank down on a milk crate. "She's only dangerous if you try to make her into something she isn't. You said it yourself, Falcon. She's not a pet."

Falcon sobbed, glaring at the dragon, who was snoring softly.

Freddy blew his nose, trying to look at Egg

objectively, like the scientist he was. The dragon was growing fast. Freddy thought she must weigh more than thirty pounds. He took out the little book he always carried and began to make tiny, precise notes. He wrote, "Dragon has reached adolescence. First kill. Ingested entire bird, feathers & all—does she have gizzard?" There was a tearstain over the "b" in "bird."

"Dragons come for a reason," said Aunt Emily. "But I don't understand this. I wish you'd never found that egg, Falcon."

Falcon turned on her fiercely. "I'm glad I did. I love Egg, no matter what she does!"

"She's a dragon, Falcon." Aunt Emily walked slowly to the pile of coats and began to put on her things. She looked sad and terribly old.

Freddy hunkered down beside Falcon. He picked up an acorn that lay beside the dragon's foot and turned it in his fingers. "Falcon," he said, after a while, "how high does she go?"

"How did you know?" said Falcon.

"There are no oak trees on this roof. How high?"

"Twenty feet, to the end of her chain," said Falcon. "She likes it."

"You still want to keep her, after what she did? She'll do it again. She has to."

"I don't care. I love her!"

Freddy put the acorn into her palm, and stood up. "I'll get a cab, Emily," he said. He took her arm and they walked toward the elevator. Just as they reached the doorway, Freddy turned. "Will you be all right? I'll be right back."

"Okay," said Falcon. She could still smell burned feathers, and she thought she might throw up. The heat warmed her face as she stared at the sleeping dragon. She saw that the collar had chafed Egg's neck as she had strained to fly higher, and the raw, angry flesh was swollen against the steel. Falcon was trying to watch Egg without looking at the sore place. She began to pick at the cuticle of her left thumb. She had a sore place too, near the base of the nail.

Above the netting that covered the roof, a flock of pigeons whirled and settled under the eaves, making "phrrt phrrt" sounds. The wind had stripped the last leaves from the trees, and their branches rattled like bones. The hum of traffic rose faintly to the tower roof, broken by an occasional horn bleep, or the whine of a siren. One of the pigeons, torn from the flock by the wind, found her balance on the east side of the museum and settled on Roosevelt's bronze head. Behind him, the old building vibrated with the tread of schoolchildren and teachers, tourists, assorted scientists, and old men and women, who regained a part of their childhood when they entered its halls. In the tower, the dragon huffed sleepily, and settled onto her sand bed. She was dreaming of things she had never seen.

Falcon got up, and fetched a pair of oven mitts from the pile near the door. She knelt again beside Egg, and tried to undo the collar, but the mitts were too big and clumsy.

The dragon stirred, and opened a turquoise eye. "Mrp?" she said sleepily.

Falcon pulled off the oven mitts. Then she took hold of the collar, unfastened it, and dropped it quickly beside Egg's foot. Each of her fingers was branded with a deep red welt. She curled her hands against her body and began to cry, tears sizzling as they splashed on the dragon's hide.

"Woorf?" said Egg anxiously, catching tears on her long blue tongue, and scrambling to her feet. She saw the collar lying by her foot and nosed it, puzzled. The dragon shook her head, and tried to reach her sore neck with her tongue.

Freddy returned to the roof just as Falcon dropped the collar.

"It hurts," she said. "Oh it hurts."

"First-aid kit," said Freddy, and went to get it.

There was nothing in it but some old Band-Aids that had had coffee spilled on them, half a roll of butter-rum Lifesavers, and a crumpled tube of Bactine. Freddy dabbed some of that on Falcon's hands and, gingerly, onto the dragon's neck. He gave himself and Falcon a Lifesaver, and offered the pack to the dragon, who sniffed it and said, "Poot!"

They sat for a while, sucking Lifesavers, and watching Egg, who was flapping her wings and arching her back in her usual wakeup exercise. "What if there are no other dragons? She'll be all alone," said Falcon. Freddy did not answer. "The others will want to say good-bye," she said at last.

"Would you like to invite them?" said Freddy. "It is a kind of Rite of Passage." Falcon knew about rites of passage from a movie she'd seen at the museum. They were ceremonies to mark the change from childhood to adulthood. They usually involved dancing and feasting, and scary things like killing lions or going off alone into the jungle.

"A Rite of Passage for Egg, you mean?" she asked.

"Partly," said Freddy, and smiled at her.

Falcon was exhausted, and curiously peaceful, as though she had run a marathon or climbed a mountain. She picked up Egg's collar, which had cooled off, and dropped it over the wall into the shrubbery six floors below. Then she fished in her pocket, pulled out the tower keys, and handed them to Freddy. "Will you help me write the invitations?" she said.

Freddy wanted to have the ceremony in the tower, because it was the safest place. But Falcon knew it had to be on the Great Lawn, where she had found Egg in the first place.

They spent the rest of the morning writing invitations, on elegant letterhead paper from Freddy's desk, with red pen. Falcon did all the writing on the final copies because Freddy's writing was so tiny you could barely make it out. Her hands hurt, and she had to wash the Bactine off so she could write, but at last they were done and put into envelopes. They said: "Please come to a Rite of Passage for Egg. 4 a.m. Meet inside park entrance West 77th Street." Falcon wrote the names of the Friends of Egg in big red letters on the envelopes. "I'll take this to Emily," said Freddy. "You deliver the rest."

"Okay," said Falcon, and looked at the stacked envelopes: Mr. Tudor Falcon Davies, Ms. Ardene Louise Taylor, Miss Emily Falcon Meade. She picked up the pen, wrote out one more invitation, folded it, and slid it into an envelope. She wrote, "Ms. Margaret

Falcon—open after Toody in bed," and sealed it. Then she went back to number 16, and up to Ardene's.

Ardene opened the door and saw Falcon standing there, her face streaked with tears and ink. "Falcon! Have you been in an accident? What on earth's the matter? What's this?" She took the invitation and read it. Her eyebrows went up so high they disappeared into her bangs. "Rite of Passage?" She peered more closely at Falcon. "What is going on, Falcon. Are you all right?"

"Yes, yes, only please come, Ardene. It's important, please?" said Falcon, pressing her mittens together, even though it hurt.

"I guess it is, baby. Sure, don't worry. I'll come, 4 a.m., good Lord."

Falcon went home and gave Missy and Toody their invitations. Toody could read letters and quite a few words.

"That's not how you spell 'right,' " he said.

"It's a different kind of rite," said Falcon. "It's kind of a . . . ceremony."

Missy stared at her envelope. "Very mysterious! What does it mean, bird?"

"I'll explain later, I promise," she said. Missy rubbed

her thumb over one of the smudges on Falcon's face. She looked puzzled, but she didn't argue.

That night, after dinner, when Toody was in bed with Henry curled on the pillow behind his head, Missy came into Falcon's room. Falcon was sitting on the bed looking out the window. The moon and Venus, the Evening Star, were visible in the clear night sky, and the window was open a crack, so the room smelled of winter. Missy settled in beside her, cuddled up under the comforter, and they sat for a while watching the sky.

Missy took the invitation out of her bathrobe pocket and opened it. "It's just the same as Toody's," she said. "Who is Egg?"

Falcon took a deep breath, smelling the night air and Missy's shampoo. Then she began to tell the whole story of Egg, beginning with that April day, seven months before, in Central Park. She told about Aunt Emily's dragons, and the tower roof, and even about her secret walks at night. Her mother's blue eyes opened wider as she listened. When Falcon came to the part about Rothschild, she choked up and stopped. Missy put an arm around her and stroked her hair.

"I think Emily tried to tell Peter and me about her dragons. It was when things began to go wrong, before Toody was born. But we were so busy fighting, we didn't listen."

Falcon wiped her eyes, and told about deciding to let Egg go, all except the part about burning her hands. She didn't want Missy to be mad at the dragon before she met her. The telling had taken a long time, and the bedside clock said 11:18 p.m.

Missy read her invitation again, and her face lit up with excitement. "A Rite of Passage!" she said. "I'll set the alarm for three fifteen. Should we dress up?"

Falcon looked at her, surprised. Dressing up was a good idea.

"Yesss . . . but not like Halloween. More like . . . church."

"Church!" said her mother. They didn't go to church, but Falcon had gone to midnight mass at St. Patrick's Cathedral with Aunt Emily the year before, and to a gospel service with Ardene.

Before she went to bed, Missy got out her dark-red velvet dress with the long, puffy sleeves that made her look like a princess in a fairy tale, and brought Falcon the big Spanish shawl that Aunt Emily had brought back from Madrid. It was real yellow silk, embroidered all over with flowers. She laid it over a chair, and bent down to give Falcon a good-night kiss. "Star light, star bright, first star I've seen tonight," Missy said, looking out at Venus. She smiled down at her daughter. "I wish Peter could be here, to meet your little dragon."

"Me too," said Falcon.

She lay in bed looking out the window at the moon. She wondered if the dragons that Aunt Emily had seen so long ago were still around, and whether Egg would ever find them. Where would they have gone? Were they all dead? And where would Egg go, and would she always be alone? "Egg, I mean," she said aloud into the silent room.

CHAPTER SEVENTEEN

She must have fallen asleep, sitting up against the pillows, because she awoke to the sound of the alarm with her neck stiff on one side. Her mother came in wearing the red velvet dress, and said, "Button me at the top, will you, bird? Are you awake?"

"Yes," she said, and buttoned the top buttons with the very tips of her burned fingers.

Missy hadn't combed her hair yet, and it was all twisted up anyhow on top of her head, with stray wisps hanging down along the back of her neck. Her neck looked as white and babyish as Toody's, only cleaner, and her skin had a hot, spicy smell, like cinnamon and roasted orange. She had a tiny crystal flask in her hand full of amber liquid.

"Mmmm," said Falcon, sniffing.

"Want some? I call it 'Dark Fire,' " said her mother, holding out the flask.

Falcon shook her head. She didn't want to smell like anything but herself. She put on the embroidered dress that her father had sent her from India. It was green and purple and had little bits of mirror sewn into the skirt and sleeves. Then Falcon brushed her hair till it shone and tied the Spanish shawl over one shoulder, which looked, she thought, perfectly elegant. She went in to wake Toody.

He was already up. He had on his new school pants and shirt, a clip-on bowtie, and the Australian hat his father had given him. "Is it time for the show?" he asked.

"It's not a show, Tood. It's Egg. Egg is going away." The words felt thick and lumpy in her throat.

"Why?" asked Toody.

"She's too big to keep. She has to go where there's room for dragons."

"Australia?" said Toody. He knew Australia had lots of room. His father had sent many pictures of the Outback. It was just miles and miles of brown land with nothing on it but a scrubby tree here and there, and a sky that went on forever.

"I don't know," said Falcon. "Maybe." Suddenly she thought Australia might not be a bad place for dragons, and she wondered whether her father would see them flying across the endless sky.

They put on their coats, scarves, and mittens. "Be very quiet," said Missy. "We don't want to wake everyone in the building."

They tiptoed down the hall and into the elevator. Enrico's eyes almost popped out of his head to see the three of them, all bundled up, walking across the lobby.

"Geez! Ms. Falcon, everything okay?" he said to Missy.

"Oh yes," she said, waving her hand in its red wool glove. "Fine. We're on a special mission."

"Holy cow!" said Enrico, and opened the door. "You be careful," he said, locking the door behind them.

Falcon led the way toward Central Park West, and across the street to the park entrance.

Aunt Emily was there, and Ardene, in a shiny gold dress under her down coat. Freddy had put on a dinner jacket and black bowtie, but hadn't been able to tie it. His overcoat was missing a button.

Aunt Emily wore a blue wool cloak with a hood, and carried her best gold-headed cane. She greeted Missy, and kissed her on the cheek.

Missy said hello to Emily and Ardene.

"This is Dr. Fernando Maldonado," said Ardene.

Freddy stared. He thought Falcon's mother looked like a princess with her crimson dress and starry blue eyes.

Missy wasn't paying any attention to him because just then she saw Egg, who was bigger than she had expected, and much hotter. Her scales caught the light from every star in the sky, and threw it back magnified. She glittered with heat. Missy screamed, thrust Falcon and Toody behind her, tried to back away, and fell into a bush.

"OH GOD! OH GOD! IT'S ON FIRE!!"

"No it's not, it's okay," said Falcon. "It's just Egg."

Missy gave a stifled squeak. Egg sat on her haunches, her eyes half closed with ecstasy. She had never smelled anything so delicious as this new and noisy person.

"It's quite safe, Ms. Falcon," said Freddy. "She's very friendly. Falcon raised her from an egg. Drakon Derkesthai, you know, the Seeing One. She has great courage, your daughter."

Missy scrambled out of the bush, and stared with all her might. "A real dragon!" she said.

"It's time to go," said Falcon, and, as though she understood, Egg set out through the snow, with

Falcon behind her. The others followed, walking on the path scorched dry by the dragon's tail.

It was a clear, cold winter's night, and the moonlight turned the snowy park into a magical place of sparkling white shapes and blue shadows. They went slowly because of Aunt Emily, and a cloud of fog rose around them as the dragon passed over the snow. As they approached the Great Lawn, they heard something and stopped for a moment to listen. It was the sound of horns and cymbals, faint and pure in the stillness of the night. The music surrounded them as they reached the edge of the lawn, which looked much larger by moonlight.

Egg started to run, but the drifts were so deep that she stumbled. "Garumph!" she said, rearing back, and snorted a great blast of fire into the whiteness. Clouds of steam billowed up, and when they cleared, there was a broad dry path leading into the very center of the Great Lawn. The dragon galloped ahead, with Falcon running after her. When they reached the middle, Egg stopped, and turned. "Mrph?" she said, looking into Falcon's eyes. The music paused, trembling on one high, sweet note. Falcon knelt beside Egg.

"It's okay," she said. "You can fly as high as you

like. You can find the other dragons." Falcon gazed into the depths of the dragon's sea-green eyes, and saw herself reflected, unique and shining with her own special magic. She stared and stared, at first because she wanted to, and then because she couldn't bear to let Egg go. At last she stood up.

"Good-bye, Egg," she said, and stepped back to make room. All around them, the music began again.

Egg unfurled her wings and shook them to get the kinks out, looking up at the moon. Arching her long neck, she gave the dragon call to the sky, and the music answered, rising into the night, glorious and triumphant.

Then the dragon stretched up on all fours, her talons barely touching the ground, like a ballerina on point. She twisted her neck around to look one last time at the six who stood together, watching. Her wings thrust down, once, and she rose into the air, slowly, easily, and circled not ten feet above their heads. With hind legs extended, forefeet curled against her chest, her powerful wings beat steadily, lifting her up and up.

"Egg!" cried Falcon. "Good-bye, Egg!"

Seeming not to hear, the dragon flew higher, streaking bright as a comet, closer and closer to the shining moon. It looked as though she would crash right into it, but at the last moment she veered, so just the tip of her wing grazed it as she passed. They heard a clear ringing sound like the chime of a tiny bell, and something fell tinkling at Falcon's feet. She bent and picked it up. "It's a ring," she said. So it was, small and bright silver, still warm with dragonfire. Falcon turned it in her hand as the others gathered around to look.

"Moonsilver," whispered Aunt Emily.

Missy took the ring from her daughter, and gasped when she saw the burns on Falcon's hands. Missy's eyes filled with tears, and she touched her lips gently to the red marks.

"Oh, my dearest bird," she said, and slipped the ring onto Falcon's finger. Hand in hand, they looked up to see the dragon rising higher and higher into the night. The others drew near, and together they stood, the six Friends, faces raised to the dragon's flight, following the flaming wings as they beat steadily against the winter sky.

Egg soared above them in great, joyful, sweeping circles, and then flew south, strong and alone, lighting the way with her own fire.